End Plan

Cameron P. Stevenson

Cover by Wendy Stevenson

ISBN: 978-0-9952902-1-1

I'd like to express my sincere thanks to the people who made End Plan possible and perhaps just a little bit more authentic feeling:

Major (retired) Philip Bury, Royal Canadian Regiment, my old friend who also served as my "go to authority" for all things military, and who spent (probably) far too much time helping me explore scenarios that popped randomly into my head.

Leanne Stinson, for her editing prowess and relentless enthusiasm.

Ron Beam, for reaching (far) back in time to his service on USS *Enterprise* to help me capture the feeling of a carrier. COD is now one of my favorite acronyms.

Dr. Geoff Peters, for answering my (likely disturbing) medical questions without batting an eye.

The folks at the **Canadian Forces Museum of Aerospace Defence** at **22 Wing/CFB North Bay, Ontario** for spending time with me talking about the Hole, and just generally having a "can do" attitude.

And finally, my wife **Wendy Stevenson** for too many things to possibly list.

Cam Stevenson
Oxford Station, Ontario
February 2017

CHAPTER ONE

Flight

The man stood at the edge of the ocean and gazed out over the grayish-blue water, the sound of the waves hitting the beach around him steady and hypnotic. The beach was long and narrow, following the curve of the shoreline in both directions as far as the eye could see, weaving gently in and out of tiny bays, a ribbon of vaguely reddish sand set against the green of lush grasses and wildflowers of white, yellow and purple. There were still several hundred more miles he needed to travel before he'd reach safety, but the flight of the last few days had taken their toll and he badly needed to rest.

Maybe they wouldn't actually make it this far, he thought, trying to convince himself of that possibility, but knowing deep down that they undoubtedly would.

He hadn't rested since just after the New Brunswick border with Quebec, where he'd managed to catch a few hours of sleep in one of the tents that the Maine National Guard had set up just south of the barricade.

A barricade manned by normally cheerful and friendly Acadians, now grim faced and clutching their hunting rifles tightly, city cops from the nearby town of Edmundston still holding on to the hope that they'd be able to keep their quiet town intact, and Guardsmen from across the river, all concerns about passports and international borders forgotten in the shared drive to stop what was coming out of the West.

He'd expected the barricade, riding down highway 185. By now he'd developed a sense of where frightened townspeople and local law enforcement tended to place them. Although what was coming wasn't using motor vehicles to travel — yet, anyway — he'd already narrowly missed being shot by an overly tense citizen-turned-soldier and had developed a technique that seemed to be working, where he simply honked his horn repeatedly as he approached. It seemed silly but for whatever reason, it worked.

Those guarding the barricades were always hungry for information, and he provided what he could. The cops from Edmundston had grilled him hard, as cops tended to do, hoping, perhaps, that if they asked him the same question in different ways that they'd get a different answer. They didn't. He liked the cops, still trying to project a sense of law and order in the face of impossible odds, still wearing their uniforms with some unconscious hope that what was on its way would show some respect for them.

Since he'd left that barricade, he'd stuck to the secondary roads and seen few people, which was just fine with him. His early experience with the main highways had depressed him — miles of asphalt clogged with hundreds of cars, all heading blindly in one direction: away. He knew that those desperate people didn't have a chance. That the areas that the government said they would hold would be overrun, and that the single one that could, and would, be held would be denied to them; neither the transportation, food or even basic lodging available. They would be turned away if they managed to make it that far and would perish in the onslaught.

The man knew this because he'd been one of those who'd drafted the Plan, and had signed his name to it. And he couldn't look at them and so traveled onward on roadways where he wouldn't have to.

He decided he'd camp where he was for the night and began to go about the business of setting up his tent. He chose a spot far enough back from the beach where his camp wouldn't be visible to others who were traveling these same secondary roads — most being honest people smart enough to realize the futility of attempting the main highways, but some looking for prey. Opportunistic fools seeking to rob travelers of their possessions, not smart enough to realize how useless those things would be in a matter of days.

The man had had a run in with some of these human jackals some hundreds of miles back, and had lost his motorcycle and the small amount of cash he was carrying. He'd managed to hang on to his ID and the USB stick he carried on a chain around his neck. Both would be critical soon. He gave up everything else without a fuss, glad to see the highwaymen disappear in search of other unwary travelers, satisfied in their haul. The man had simply walked the few miles to a dealership he'd seen on the way and taken another motorcycle. The highwaymen were now undoubtedly absorbed into the oncoming wave. He was certain that they were too stupid to avoid it.

He'd also picked up a revolver and ammunition, almost on a whim, at a sporting goods store near the dealership. Time was running out, he thought, and he wouldn't be able to keep replacing his transportation if he wanted to make it in time. He'd prefer to avoid using it, which is why he was careful in the choice of his camp sites. He would use it if he had to, though. He'd spent a few minutes coming to that decision before shoving the gun into his pack.

He'd become quite good at setting up and tearing down his simple camp and soon had the tent set up, the sleeping bag inside it and the single burner butane stove running with his aluminum camp kettle on top, boiling water for tea and washing up. He'd eat a cold meal tonight. He had neither the energy to prepare anything substantial nor the desire to eat it. Food was simply the fuel his body needed to keep going.

He saw the flash on the horizon to the West at dusk as he sat drinking his cooling tea, having finished the dried meats, cheese and bread that served as his dinner. He looked at his watch instinctively and noted the time. He continued to drink his tea, and felt the rumble minutes later. He looked at his watch and did the mental calculation. Chicago, he thought. This was in the Plan too, but it was being done earlier than he expected. He needed to get on the road at dawn, he thought, and tossed the remainder of his tea into the nearby grasses, rinsed his cup and crawled into his tent for another night of troubled sleep.

The man came across the young mother and her son early the next morning near Alma. Her car had broken down the previous evening and she and the boy — two or three years old, he thought — had slept in the car, sheltered from the chill of the Atlantic night. The residents of the area had moved on and tourists were non-existent, now driving for their lives rather than to the next attraction.

He saw the woman sitting, crying, as he slowed down to go around her car and instead found himself pulling over rather than accelerating and leaving her and her problems behind him. It was one thing to leave the masses of humanity on the highways to their doom — he couldn't save them all. It was stupidly sentimental, he thought, given the stakes involved, but he could help this one person, and that was something. Still, he wasn't a complete fool and he jammed the revolver down the back of his pants as he got off his bike and walked towards her and her child.

The woman was young, no more than a girl really. The man thought she was in her early twenties, maybe twenty-one or twenty-two. She was pretty, slim with long dark hair and blue eyes red-rimmed from crying. The man thought she would almost be beautiful if she smiled. Her son took after her in looks, with the same dark hair and blue eyes, and he sat in the back seat of the car playing with some toy dinosaurs. The boy looked up at the man as he approached, but saw nothing interesting and returned to his toys. The mother had watched the man with a wary gaze the whole time he walked from his motorcycle. The man thought that she most likely had a weapon — a knife probably, not a gun. He imagined he looked a bit disreputable from his hard ride, and didn't blame her for her suspicion.

"Car trouble, I take it?" he asked when he came close enough to talk to the woman without yelling.

"Yes," she replied, "it just stopped as I was driving along, and I managed to pull over, but I have no idea what the problem is, and I need to meet my husband."

The man nodded. "I can look at it if you like."

"Oh yes, please," said the woman, suspicion momentarily forgotten in her rising hope.

"Keys?"

"In the ignition."

The woman moved out of the way to give him access to the driver's side of the car. The man noticed the small knife she moved to her pocket. He turned the ignition key and received nothing — no bells, lights or engine cranking. He popped the hood and got out of the car, walked to the front and opened it. After a few minutes with his head under the hood peering into the dark corners of the engine compartment he found what he was looking for. Reaching in and following the thick wire to its source, he felt what he had expected. He stood straight and turned to the woman, now standing near him.

"Do you have a wrench? Any kind of crescent wrench will do."

"Do you know what the problem is?" she asked with optimism.

"Loose grounding wire," replied the man, "the rough roads can work them loose."

"And you can fix it?"

"If you have a wrench, I can tighten it up and everything should be fine. I can hand tighten it, but it'll just work itself loose after a few miles."

"There're some tools in the back."

She led him to the trunk and opened it. Sure enough there was a small roadside emergency kit. Probably a present from someone concerned with this young mother driving alone on country roads with her son. The man thought that that person would be happy knowing how useful it had ended up being.

He found what he needed quickly and returned to the engine compartment, tightening the bolt holding the grounding strap. The car started immediately when he tried it. The boy looked up from his toys and clapped his hands with a broad smile on his face. The man closed the hood and returned the wrench to its place in the emergency kit.

"Oh my God, thank-you," said the woman, who had stood back and watched the man as he made the repair.

"You're welcome," he replied, satisfied that he had helped at least one person in his flight.

"I don't know how to thank you. In fact, I don't even know your name. I'm Mary, and my son's name is Joshua." She offered her hand. The man took it, and told her his own name.

Mary's husband, it turned out, was a soldier who had been deployed days earlier when the proverbial shit had hit the fan. He had had some inkling of how bad things were going to get, and had given his wife instructions to keep to the secondary roads. Exactly the way the man was traveling. In fact, they were traveling to the same destination. However the man knew, as Mary's husband didn't, that she would be turned back. It was in the Plan.

He made a snap decision.

"I'm on my way to Sydney as well," he said, "if you like, we can travel together. It might be safer that way, especially if you have more car problems." The man didn't mention the fact that this would also be her only way of getting through. It would involve more explaining than he wanted to do.

Mary searched his face before replying, suspicious once again.

"Are you going to keep riding your motorcycle?" she asked, still not trusting him enough to have him in the car with her and her son, with no options for escape should he turn out to be something other than what she thought he was.

"I'd prefer to," replied the man.

Mary nodded. "Okay, let's get going then."

That night found the three of them camped out off the road, a couple of hundred miles closer to their destination. The man gave the tent to Mary and her son along with his sleeping bag. He would be okay catching whatever sleep he could in the front seat of her car. He wasn't sleeping very well anyway.

He decided to risk a small fire that night. The air was chill blowing in from the ocean, and they could use the warmth. That was his story, in any case. The fact of the matter was that he found the flames comforting. A bit of homeyness in a desperate situation.

As they sat around the fire, Joshua nestled against his mother's side, her arm around him, with the glazed look of a child who is fighting sleep, there were three more flashes on the horizon. One in the West, and two towards the South.

"I saw one of those the other night," said Mary, "do you know what they are?"

"Nuclear sterilization," replied the man absently, as he checked the time on his watch. "Toronto, New York and Boston is my guess."

"What?" she asked incredulously.

The rumbles minutes later confirmed his guess and the man suddenly realized that he had just given away more than he should have. So far, he had been able to fob off Mary's questions about his own situation with vagaries. He supposed it didn't matter, that she'd find out tomorrow anyway. And it would be a relief to tell his story to another human being.

"Nuclear sterilization. A nice clean clinical term for incinerating cities full of people. Each of those flashes is a nuclear warhead being detonated over a major city. An air burst, mind you, for maximum effect."

Mary stared at him in shock for a moment and then slowly shook her head. "No. I can't believe that. Everything was fine just a few days ago. They must be something else."

The man continued.

"I was working in a government lab trying to find a cure. We knew about the virus about two weeks before it started manifesting itself in a way that was noticeable to the public. You remember the small riots that seemed to spring up and were explained away as student protests gone bad?"

Mary nodded, still struggling to come to grips with the enormity of what the man was telling her.

"That was the start. We managed to control those — barely — but the virus spread. All it needs is for some bodily fluid to be transferred. A bite or a scratch is most likely, but even something as innocent as a kiss before symptoms start to show. When things started to come apart, we directed people to safe zones that could possibly be defended. You know all about that, but your husband was smart enough to send you elsewhere. Everyone underestimated how fast it would spread and how uncontrollable the infected are. The safe zones didn't last long."

"But nuking cities? My God, I can't believe that. It's insane."

"There was a lot of discussion about it. I was against it: there's a chance that the radiation on the outskirts of the blasts could cause mutation of the virus. It isn't airborne right now, for example. Things would be a lot more hopeless if it was. It looks like they decided to do it anyway though. They're probably trying to protect whatever safe zones are left by burning out millions of infected like you would hornet nests. I don't know for sure though, I haven't talked to anyone in authority since I left."

"I was the last one out," he continued, "everyone else was evacuated days before, but I thought I was on to something so I kept at it. I didn't know what the equipment would be like in the new labs, and I wanted to get as far as I could. When I left, I could hear the infected blocks away."

There was a long silence when the man finished his story. He wondered if he had told the woman too much, if she would think him one of those responsible for what was happening and hate him for it.

"Did you find a cure?" asked Mary finally.

The man shook his head slowly. "I don't know. I don't think there's a cure...any way to revert the infected back to who they used to be...there's too much damage. But maybe a vaccine. If the virus doesn't mutate." He looked at the three dying glows on the horizon as he said this, each representing the remote-control cremation of what used to be cities of millions of people.

Mary followed his gaze.

"You at least need to try," she said, hugging her now sleeping son to her tightly.

Next morning, they came across the first real authority the man had seen in days. Soldiers had barricaded the causeway that would carry them on the final leg of their journey to safety, two armored personnel carriers sitting in the road, their cannon pointed menacingly at any who approached. Behind them, soldiers moved busily amongst troop carriers and jeeps, and in front of them, a handful armed with rifles turned back those travelers who approached, forcing them to perform U-turns and return back down the causeway.

The man pulled up in the line of cars and campers leading to the barricade, with Mary's car behind him. He turned and looked at her, seeing the concern in her face. He raised his hand slightly to signal her not to worry. Ahead of him, he watched as an argument ensued between a soldier and the driver of a pickup truck brimming with household belongings. The man was transfixed by the sight of the items that the driver thought were important enough to bring with him. He found the elaborate gas barbecue particularly fascinating.

It was clear that the driver wasn't happy at being turned back. As the argument grew more heated, two other troopers strode over and leveled their rifles at the driver through the windshield. The driver seemed to get the message at this point and put his truck in gear, performing a wide U-turn, narrowly avoiding the first soldier.

The rest of the vehicle owners in the line ahead of the man, having witnessed the altercation ahead of them, meekly turned around when each was ordered to. Eventually it was the man's turn.

"I'm sorry, sir, but you'll have to turn around. No civilian vehicles are allowed beyond this point."

"I'm on your list," the man said calmly.

"I'm not aware of any list, sir. You'll have to turn around now."

"Get whoever is in charge over here. You really don't want to turn me back."

The soldier hesitated, then decided to pass the buck up the ranks.

"Wait here, sir."

The man shut off the motorcycle and waited for several minutes until the soldier returned with a sergeant carrying a clipboard.

"Your name?" asked the sergeant.

The man gave him his name and the sergeant checked the list attached to the clipboard. It was pitifully short, consisted of two pages of double spaced text. The sergeant found the man on the second page.

"You're a bit late, sir," said the sergeant, "we're about to blow the causeway and fold operations here. If you'd got here tomorrow you'd be swimming."

"It's been a tough ride," replied the man. "How far away are they?"

"Moncton's gone," said the sergeant, "another day or two and we expect them here. The general evacuation order's been given and we're heading out as soon as we set the charges."

The man thought of the group of civilians, cops and Guardsmen back at Edmundston. He'd liked them and

16

their determination and hoped that they'd somehow managed to get away.

"How's the road up to Sydney?" the man asked.

"It should be fine," replied the sergeant. "None of the infected, if that's what you mean, but I'd watch out for the folks who've decided to take things into their own hands. You're welcome to travel with us, if you like."

"I need to get this information to St. John's," replied the man, taking the chain holding the USB stick out of his shirt and showing it to the sergeant. "Time is, as they say, of the essence."

"A plane sure would be useful, wouldn't it?" asked the sergeant.

Nothing had been in the air for the past two weeks but fighter jets enforcing the no-fly zone over North America, directed by the joint command safely buried under a mountain. There was no negotiating with the fighter pilots, and no exceptions. The man had seen evidence of this several times in his travels in the form of metal, plastic and bodies strewn over the landscape as private and commercial pilots decided to try their luck. It was in the Plan, and it didn't surprise him when he saw it.

"It sure would," replied the man, "I think I'm getting saddle sores."

The sergeant laughed. "Well, good luck, sir."

The man nodded and started the motorcycle, accelerating slowly up the narrow path leading through the military encampment. He looked for Mary in the rear-view mirror and saw that she'd been stopped by the soldiers. He doubled back to where she was stopped. He left the bike running and got off and walked over to the car.

"She's with me," he said to the sergeant, who hadn't returned to whatever he had been doing before the man had arrived.

"She isn't on the list."

"No."

"Well, I really shouldn't let her through if she's not on the list."

The man stared at him without saying anything. Eventually the sergeant dropped his eyes and sighed, then looked back at the man.

"I guess it doesn't really matter, does it? Go on then."

The man got back on his bike and started it, and waved to Mary to follow him, their successful passage giving vain hope to the others in the line behind them. The soldiers' job would be harder for a little while. The tiny convoy threaded its way through the troops before hitting the open causeway and the man accelerated, eager to put the blockade behind him before someone higher up than the sergeant decided to stop them.

They arrived at the ferry that afternoon. The winding mountainous road had been empty — the inhabitants along the way having fled or holed up, hoping that the tide wouldn't come or would pass them by. It was rough country, and the man thought that they might have a chance if they were careful.

Enough of the locals had had the same idea of trying to leave the mainland that the marshaling yard was a sea of vehicles, the entrance road impassable for the cars and trucks jammed into it. The man rode to a stop at the end of the line far, far from the ferry, and motioned Mary to pull alongside him. The air was heavy with the smell of dead fish and diesel fuel.

"You'll have to ride with me," he yelled over the sound of his engine after she rolled down her window, "there's no way we're getting through this with a car."

"But Joshua…"

"Get on the back and put him between us. You can hold onto me with one arm and him with the other. We're not going to be going fast."

Mary nodded, switched off the car and got out. She hurried to the back door and extracted Joshua from his car seat, grabbing her purse, which lay beside the boy, almost as an afterthought. The man resumed surveying the activity closer to the ferry and felt Mary get on behind him. He glanced over his shoulder and saw Joshua looking up at him smiling. He smiled back and then looked directly at Mary.

"Ready?"

"Go."

The man put the bike in gear and inched it forward, weaving between cars and onto the shoulder, taking whatever path he could to make it down to the boat. He saw soldiers in the distance and made for them.

Behind him he could hear yelling as outraged drivers, hoping in vain to get on the ship that would take them to safety, watched him jump the queue. He ignored them and continued in the direction of the troops, who were now taking an interest in his approach.

He felt the impact of the bullet before he heard the shot, and managed to bring the bike to a stop. He looked down and saw the blood beginning to soak the front of his shirt. At least it missed the USB stick, he thought.

He got off the motorcycle shakily and stood to face Mary, her questioning look changing to one of horror as she saw what had happened. She dismounted quickly, pulling Joshua off with her, and ran over to him as he sank to the ground.

He pulled the chain with the USB stick over his head and handed it to her, and then dug in his pocket for his ID and gave her that as well. As his vision began to fade, he saw the soldiers running towards them.

"Make sure they get this," he said to her, as darkness engulfed him.

CHAPTER TWO

Mary

Mary stepped out of the house and closed the door behind her, pulling it tight and making sure it was latched before starting the walk to her job. The day was bright and sunny and almost cloudless, the ever-present wind blowing in from the ocean ruffling her hair and clothes as soon as she stepped out of the shelter of the house. She remembered to pull up her mask, covering her nose and mouth.

The wind brought fallout with it. So far nothing else.

She walked down the narrow streets of the town as she did every morning, heading in the direction of the docks. It was a small town and she didn't mind the walk. Not that it mattered; she didn't own a car and even if she did, there wasn't any gas to buy. Everyone walked these days except for the military and emergency responders. From the talk she'd heard in the college's cafeteria, it wouldn't be too long before the latter group would be walking too.

In another time, she would have found the town charming. Small frame houses painted in a riot of different colors, built wherever there'd been a flat place to put them. It was cozy and quaint, a picture postcard, tainted by the knowledge of the nearby camp and all of its implications. She'd rather be here though. Rumors of trouble in the larger towns and cities — St. John's and Corner Brook mostly — had reached the town. Too many people and not enough food. The Americans in Gander seemed to be doing better; the massive airlift in the final days ensured that they had enough supplies. At least for a while.

There was almost no activity on the streets. Most people had nowhere to go and preferred to stay inside where they felt they were safe. The virus was a thing of the mainland to most of them, but the fallout was real. The college monitored it and supplied advisories that the local radio station broadcast three times a day, along with pop music and scant news updates, read by DJs who struggled to put some semblance of normality into their voices. Mary could have done without the music. It seemed ludicrous.

As she walked, she wondered what job they'd put her to today. It was clearly make-work. A gift bestowed upon her, along with the room in which she and Joshua lived, by appreciative authorities. After which they promptly forgot about her. Still, she was grateful for both, not to mention the older woman who owned the house and who looked after Joshua during the day. The alternative would have been the camp, like the other mothers and children she saw every day. She shuddered at the thought.

Before long, Mary rounded a corner and the camp came into sight. From the distance, it could have been the scene of a county fair: a sea of tents large and small, both green utilitarian army issue and others that were clearly intended for use in happier times, arranged in an orderly grid, people wandering the paths between them as if they were out for a stroll. The illusion was spoiled as she came closer and the surrounding fence became apparent. Closer still and the smell hit her for a moment, carried by a change in the fickle wind. The mask helped with that too.

She steeled herself as she walked down the access road to the agriculture inspection station that had been repurposed for processing and which was the only point of access to the fenced in area.

The camp had replaced the ferry in Mary's nightmares, although the latter still sometimes made a guest appearance. The pills that came in the little paper cup along with the dinner rations helped dim the horrors that she and everyone else from away had experienced, but they couldn't banish them completely.

She'd tried to put the ferry out of her mind and instead focus on the jobs they gave her. That and on Joshua, who mercifully was too young to realize what was going on. At least she hoped he was. He seemed okay, but she still worried about him.

Just seeing the big ship docked outside the camp was often enough to cause a crippling flood of memories.

The soldiers rushing her on board, one of them carrying Joshua and one of them with the man's body in a fireman's carry. Other troops returning fire at the men in the crowd who'd decided to make use of the hunting rifles they'd brought with them. The crowd turning into a mob and forcing its way onto the car deck. The hurried cast off with crew desperately seeking instructions and frantic soldiers securing the ship as best they could. The endless hours of the voyage spent huddled in a lounge, covered in the man's blood and clutching Joshua to her. The mob destroying everything they could in an attempt to gain access to the rest of the ship. And finally, the troops at their destination, clearing the breached sections of the ship in a fury of lead and fire.

The smell had been worse than the screams.

Maybe more of the pills would help.

Mary entered the cavernous building and stopped at the duty desk as she did each morning. The elderly town official who manned it glanced up as she arrived and sat up, prepared for the scene that the two played out every day.

"Morning, Mary"

"Good morning, Tom. Any news?"

He nodded. "Some. Nothing really concrete. We found out that your husband's unit is supposed to be in Labrador. The military isn't completely sure; things are still pretty messed up. No more details than that I'm afraid."

"Labrador?"

"Goose Bay. They're trying to keep it open. But like I said, they're not entirely sure. They said they're trying to confirm." He smiled wryly. "It isn't exactly their highest priority."

"Anyway, keep asking," he continued, "maybe one of these days I'll have a better answer for you."

They weren't sure, she thought. How bad are things if you can lose a whole army unit?

It was times like this that Mary missed the man most.

It wasn't Tom's fault though, and she gave him a weak smile. "It's something, Tom. Thanks for keeping at this for me." She paused, changing topics. She knew he was uncomfortable with this part of the morning's routine.

"So, what have you got for me today?"

Tom reached down beside him and pulled up what looked like a large plastic baggy filled with white pills. He put it on the desk between them.

"Potassium Iodide tablets. We got a shipment in and we're supposed to make sure that they get distributed to the refugees."

Mary recognized the tablets. The first time she'd seen the pills with her meal she'd asked a fellow diner, who looked like he might know what was going on, what they all were. She knew this one was for radiation. Joshua received half of one in his own paper cup, from which the other pills were absent.

"It's pretty simple," said Tom, "one for an adult, half for a child. None for anyone over 40. Oh, and make sure when you give them out that they get swallowed.

We don't want these turning into a trade item like the masks were."

"Got it," she replied, picking up the baggy and preparing to make her way through the building to the camp.

"Oh, and Mary..."

She stopped.

"One more thing. I'm supposed to tell you that there's an escort for you. There was trouble in the camp last night and the military wants all civilian workers to have an escort when they're inside."

"What kind of trouble?"

"A fight got out of hand. They sent in a squad. It wasn't pretty."

"That doesn't surprise me," replied Mary, "people are bored and scared. We need to get them out of that camp faster. It's only going to get worse."

He nodded. "Yeah. But we can only process them so fast. St. John's is telling us to keep a lid on things any way we can while they try to speed it up."

"Well, they better get a move on," she replied, "I don't think they have much time left."

"Don't forget your escort, Mary. I'm serious."

"I will, Tom. See you tomorrow."

"You bet."

Mary walked deeper into the big, dimly lit, industrial building towards the daylight at the other end, passing stacked boxes of supplies on her way.

Near the other side was the processing station — a long table with several chairs on one side and desktop computers on it, cables snaking down and away, secured to the floor with scuffed duct tape. This was usually the busiest place in the building, a long line of hopeful refugees in front and one of the town's three Mounties behind the table, along with a nurse and the town clerk. It was here that the authorities attempted to find a place for the refugees, outside of the camp. The locals were nothing if not hospitable, throwing open their homes to those from the mainland having nowhere else to go.

The authorities were careful in what they unleashed on an unsuspecting population though. The Mounties, with a fragile and sluggish network connection back to an abandoned Ottawa, ran background checks on servers still drawing emergency power. The nurse performed various medical checks. Including the most important one.

It was a painfully slow process and some days the line moved barely, if at all. Still, there was little else to do in the camp and people came out every morning, hoping that they'd get lucky.

Today there was no line and no one behind the table. The computers were off.

There were an abnormal number of troops in the building. Mary supposed this was due to the trouble last night. She spotted what she guessed was her escort standing beside a pillar on which was mounted a large "No Smoking" sign. There were two of them, smoking, obviously waiting for someone. She walked over, amused by the scene. People had more to care about these days than second-hand smoke.

"I take it you're my escort," she said to them as she approached. They were bulky in their combat gear, rifles slung. She couldn't resist adding: "And you have a hard time reading signs," gesturing to the one on the pillar.

The two soldiers both looked up at the sign in surprise and then, sheepishly, back at Mary. They tossed their butts on the floor, one after the other. "Sorry, ma'am," said one.

Mary knew that she'd become something of an icon to the troops. Her desperate voyage here; her blood-soaked state on arrival, clutching her son to her in an iron grip; her refusal to hand over the items that the man had entrusted her with until she was satisfied she was giving them to the right person. She could only imagine how the stories evolved. She also suspected that the soldiers kept an eye out for her hoping that in return someone out there was looking after their own young families. Wherever they were.

Mary laughed. "Don't worry about it. I'm Mary." She offered her hand to each of them in turn. They both shook it gently, as if she were some delicate flower that they'd damage. She found it charming given the circumstances.

"Uhh, we know, ma'am," said the same soldier. He seemed to be the spokesman for the pair. "We've been ordered to stay with you in the camp. I don't know if you heard, but there was some trouble last night."

"I heard," replied Mary, "and I don't really think I need an escort. Try to stay inconspicuous, will you? I mean, as inconspicuous as you can with all your gear on. People are jittery enough and the sight of you two hovering around me might keep people who need the meds away."

"Yes, ma'am," said the spokesman, "we'll stay out of your way."

She forced a bright smile. "Okay then, let's get to work. Come on."

Mary set up at the "official" table in the busy mess tent. She didn't feel very official, but she supposed that to these people she was. The table's position and lack of chairs on one side distinguished it as official; that and someone from outside the camp occasionally using it for official purposes. No one else sat at the old battered church-basement piece of furniture no matter how crowded the tent became, just in case it was needed. It was their one link to the outside.

There was a buzz of interest as Mary was setting up. This was something different in an otherwise dreary day and the refugees were excited by it. Mary took the opportunity to explain what she'd be giving out. Radiation was low on the list of concerns amongst the people in the tent, but anything that was a diversion was stimulating. Once she was ready, her escort helped organize an orderly line and then faded into the background as she'd requested.

It quickly became a social occasion as much as anything else, and each person who stood in front of her took the opportunity to press her for the little information she could provide about conditions out in the world. The rumors running through the camp astounded her.

The line in front of her table gradually moved forwards as she handed out the pills. If she was unsure about someone's age, she asked, and turned them away if they were too old. Most left without comment, still trusting authority, a few wanting to argue, which wasted time and made the others in the line irritable. She was concerned about the big rough looking character three people down in the line. She'd seen him the other day arguing with one of the Mounties. She guessed that something in his past had turned up and was preventing him from getting out of the camp, and since then he'd become one of the resident troublemakers, stirring dissent with accusations and wild theories. She pegged him for a bully as well as a loudmouth.

Soon enough he stood in front of her.

"Your age, sir?" she asked, knowing full well that he was over the limit but going through the motions anyway.

"You can't ask me that. I know my rights," he replied belligerently, clearly spoiling for a fight and wanting to put on a show for others in the line.

Mary sighed. "If you're over 40 you're not getting a pill. If you won't tell me your age you're not getting one either. There's potential for some bad side effects that outweigh the benefits."

"Do you think I'm an idiot?" he demanded, then, added loudly for his audience: "I know what you people are doing, keeping the young ones healthy so you can put them to work somewhere and letting the rest of us get sick and die."

Continuing to show off for the onlookers, he grabbed her wrist with his hand and leaned in uncomfortably close. "Now be a good girl and give me a pill, won't you?" He glanced sideways at the bag and made a grab for it. Mary deftly moved it out of his reach.

She looked over her shoulder for her escort, who she thought should have intervened by now. She saw them standing near the tent doorway, listening to their earpieces, concentration on their faces, eyes looking down rather than in her direction.

She stared back at the bully. "Take your hand off me."

He squeezed her wrist tighter in response. She felt a sharp pain but kept her face expressionless, not wanting to give him the satisfaction of a reaction. "Not until you give me what I want," he said with veiled menace, "I have all day."

Mary looked back for the soldiers again. They'd started to move in her direction, walking with clear purpose, some decision having been made. They quickly reached the table.

"We have to go," said one, the one she thought of as the spokesman.

"I seem to have a problem here, in case you didn't notice," she replied, gesturing with a tilt of her head at the troublemaker before her, still clutching her wrist while assessing the new arrivals.

The soldier reached down and forcibly removed the hand grasping her wrist. She winced at the pain.

"Hey," began the hand's owner, preparing to include the serviceman in his performance.

"Walk away, sir," said the soldier.

"Not until I..."

Almost too quickly to see, rifles were unslung and leveled.

"Walk away," the soldier repeated flatly.

Grumbling but suddenly deflated, the bully turned and slunk away, muttering in a low voice. It was clear, even to him, that the troops had little time for his antics. The spokesman slung his rifle while his partner continued to hold his own at the ready. He turned back to Mary. "We have to go."

"But I'm not done here," she replied.

"Now," stressed the soldier, grasping the same wrist that had just been released and pulling her to her feet, the refugees in the line and standing elsewhere in the tent watching with concern. Something was happening, and it didn't look like something good. The tension became palpable.

"Okay, okay, let me pack things up."

"Leave it."

The soldier began to walk towards the tent entrance with Mary in tow, followed by his partner who kept an eye on the crowd as they left, his rifle pointing at nothing in particular but giving the impression of pointing everywhere.

"Walk until we get outside," he said quietly to Mary, "then we run for all we're worth."

"What the hell is going on?" demanded Mary.

"There's an outbreak in the camp," replied the soldier, "we need to get out fast. They're only giving us a couple of minutes before they seal things off."

"Jesus."

As they reached the doorway of the tent, the first screams started from elsewhere in the camp.

"Run," said the soldier, dragging Mary with him as the refugees in the tent suddenly realized what was happening.

The camp was turning quickly to chaos as the three ran through it, aiming for the processing building and the exit. Mary tripped, unable to keep up with the soldiers' long strides and one of them picked her up and carried her. As she was bounced and jarred, she saw her first infected, overpowering others. She heard the rattle of an automatic rifle from deeper in the camp. Someone wasn't going to make it out in time.

"Almost there," yelled the soldier carrying her, breathing heavily from exertion. Another automatic rifle exploded loudly into life. It was the other member of her escort, mowing down people running towards them, his face a grim mask. Sweat beaded his forehead.

They reached the entrance to the building, blocked by a line of troops.

"Is she bit?" yelled the one that seemed to be in charge.

"She tripped."

"Go!" He gestured sharply towards the exit. "Get out of here! The planes are inbound!"

Her escort moved through the troops, who ignored them, focused on the rush of refugees and infected heading in their direction. It was impossible to tell which was which. As they passed through the building to the outside, Mary heard the gunfire begin in earnest.

"I have to put you down," said the soldier carrying her, exhausted from the run, and set her down.

"What now?" she asked.

"You heard it. Planes are inbound. We need to get clear."

"What about the troops back there? And the people in the camp?"

The two soldiers looked at each other but said nothing, panting and bent over, hands on their knees, trying to catch their breaths. A few seconds break and they led her, running again, up the access road, looking around them as if searching for something.

"This'll have to do," said one. The other nodded. Mary could hear the sound of jet engines in the distance, approaching rapidly.

He pointed. "Down here."

She followed them down the side of the road's embankment opposite to the camp, trying not to trip on the loose rocks and gravel as she descended the sharp decline.

"Get down. Cover your ears."

She heard the scream of the approaching jets and thought about the flashes, and the man's explanation of them. Surely that wasn't what was about to happen here. They wouldn't.

Mary threw herself to the dirt and weeds and covered her ears tightly with her hands. A moment later she felt a crushing weight atop her and knew that one of the soldiers was covering her with his own body. Joshua, she had time to think, please God let him be inside.

A moment later the jets passed and the world exploded.

CHAPTER THREE

Surprise Awakening

Thunder in the distance. He'd have to find a place to wait out the storm; he hated riding in the rain.

He heard the sound of people. Some crying, some yelling, some with the unmistakable tone of command, although he couldn't make out any words. Someone would make a last-ditch appeal to him at any second. Come with us, you can finish in the new labs. But he'd decline again like he had the first time. All he needed was a couple more days.

Much to his surprise, the man awoke.

He felt groggy and light headed, as if with the aftermath of a night of heavy drinking. And hungry. He didn't remember ever feeling this hungry.

He looked around and saw that he was in a hospital room, indistinguishable from any other hospital room he'd ever seen. The blinds on the room's single window were open and dim daylight streamed in. From his vantage in the bed, he couldn't see anything but a gray sky. Early afternoon, he thought. It looked like it might be drizzling outside. He wondered where he was.

He tried to sit up, with a vague thought of getting something to eat, or maybe looking out the window. The pain that hit him put an end to that idea quickly. He felt like he'd been hit by a truck. Not that he'd ever experienced that first hand, but he'd heard other people use the phrase and it seemed to him that it fit perfectly.

He saw that there were a lot of wires stuck to him, as well as an IV tube. His chest appeared to be heavily bandaged as well, but it was hard to get a close look no matter how much he bent his neck. He guessed that the monitor attached to all those wires would let a nurse know that he was awake. He wondered how long he'd have to lie here until someone came to check on him. He hoped they'd bring dinner.

The man had run out of things to look at and decided to close his eyes again when the door to his room swung open. A middle aged, serious looking nurse marched through. The man liked middle aged serious looking nurses. If he was going to be in a hospital, he wanted a middle aged serious looking nurse caring for him.

As the door eased closed behind her, he caught a glimpse of a camouflaged arm beside his door, and the hallway outside. He could see that it was packed with people; most of them visibly injured. Some badly, from what he could tell by the brief look. The door shut completely and blocked off his view. It also cut off the sobbing.

"Decided to rejoin the living, have we?", the nurse asked as she reached his bed and began to examine him.

"It seems that I have," he rasped. The sound of his voice startled him. It sounded like an old rusty gate.

"Humph. It's about time you did. You've been filling one of our only two ICU beds for long enough. Lord knows we could've used it."

The man didn't know what to say in response.

"I'm sorry."

The nurse seemed to realize that she was taking out her frustration on the wrong person.

"Well, it isn't exactly your fault I suppose. Still, you would have been all right in one of the other beds if the military would have let us move you. But when we tried, they went and posted a guard. Can you believe that? An armed guard!" She looked towards the door. "Who I should probably let know that you're awake. I'm sure your people will want to talk to you right away."

"Can you tell me where I am?" asked the man.

He was dismayed when she told him. The wrong ferry, he thought. He should be on the other side of the island.

"Well, from what I've heard, you're fortunate that you made it here at all," she said, seeing the disappointment on his face. "And we don't have a lot of experience with gunshot victims around here. You're lucky to be alive. You should be thankful for that."

The man mumbled agreement as he thought of the implications. Surely his data would have made it to St. John's even if he hadn't. The network should still be up on the island even if the mainland was out. They'd considered this when the Plan was being worked out. For the moment, however, there was nothing he could do about it.

"Any chance of something to eat?" he asked, this being only a slightly less important matter to him at the moment.

"You'll have to wait until the doctor sees you first," she replied. "He shouldn't be too long. Anyway, you seem to be doing just fine. I'll let your people know you're awake, and they can see you as soon as the doctor's done."

The nurse turned and marched out the same way that she'd marched in. The man settled back to wait.

"Shouldn't be long" turned out to be optimistic. The man had expected that. He had no way of telling time except for the quality of the daylight illuminating the room, but it seemed to him that at least an hour had passed since the nurse had left. Maybe two. He used the time to dwell on what the current situation might be. He'd managed to knot himself up badly with worry when the door to his room swung open again.

This time it was two men who walked in. In the lead was the doctor, an exhausted looking elderly man wearing a rumpled white coat. It looked like he might've been sleeping in it. Behind him was an army officer, who calmly followed the doctor into the room and stood back while the doctor approached the man. The army officer wore a haunted look.

"Let's have a look at you," said the doctor, with no preamble. He bent to examine the man's bandaged chest. "How's the pain?" he asked without looking up.

"Manageable," replied the man, "as long as I don't move."

The doctor grunted. "We don't have a lot of experience with gunshot victims around here. You're lucky to be alive."

"I've heard that."

The doctor finished his examination. A cursory one, in the man's opinion. Whatever was going on outside was obviously swamping the frail looking physician. The man thought he looked like he might be on the verge of collapse.

"You appear to be healing up just fine. I'll prescribe some pain medication, but I wouldn't suggest you do too much moving around for at least a week." He glanced at the army officer behind him. "I'd like to move him out of the ICU." The officer nodded.

"Well then. I'll check up on you again tomorrow," he said to the man. Then, turning to leave: "He's all yours, Major. Remember that he's still recovering from a very serious injury. Please don't place unnecessary stress on him."

The doctor walked past the officer and left the room.

The major approached the man's bed. The name sewn onto his uniform was "MARSHALL".

"I'm afraid the stress is going to be necessary," he said, reaching out his hand. "Harry Marshall." The man reached out and shook it and pain bloomed in his chest. "Sorry about that," said the major, seeing the expression on the man's face.

The man was impatient to start what he expected would be a briefing, but he had one priority greater than that.

"You know, I hate to ask, but the doctor was in and out so fast I didn't get a chance to find out about something to eat and drink. Any way before we get started…"

"Of course. Sorry about that, I thought that would've been taken care of before now."

"No," replied the man, "the staff seems to be preoccupied."

Marshall nodded. "We'll get to the reason for that once you've eaten." He turned and left the room. The man waited; he was doing a lot of that. Marshall returned quickly though.

"Jimmy's going to go and find you something."

Jimmy must be the owner of the camouflaged arm that the man had glimpsed earlier.

Marshall picked up a plastic chair and carried it over, setting it down facing the man. He settled into it with a sigh. The man could see the dark circles under his eyes.

"Now. Where to begin," he said.

"The data that I brought," prompted the man, this being the second most urgent concern he had.

"The data made it to St. John's. That woman that was with you…"

"Mary."

"Yes, Mary. She was quite something. Wouldn't give it up to just anyone. I had to convince her that I'd make sure it got to the lab boys immediately before she'd hand it over."

"Which you did."

"Yes. St. John's didn't want it to go over the network, so we broke protocol and put it on a chopper. We would have done the same with you but the staff here didn't think you'd make it."

"And the results? A vaccine?"

"Not from what I've heard. Not yet. Although we're having some communication issues so I don't necessarily have all the information. Still lots of confusion out there. The evacuation happened so fast. Lots of people and equipment ended up in the wrong place. But you know all about that." Marshall looked around the room meaningfully.

The man smelled the food before a young soldier — Jimmy, the man assumed — entered the room with his meal. He was wearing a sidearm.

"Ah. Thank you, Jimmy," said Marshall as the soldier handed a tray to the man.

"You're welcome, sir," he replied, "anything else I can get?"

"No, that's fine for now, son. Thank you."

The soldier saluted and left to resume his guard duty outside the man's room. The man attacked the food. It looked horrible. It tasted wonderful.

"Did you really need to post a guard?" asked the man between bites.

Marshall nodded grimly. "I'm afraid so. The hospital staff is overwhelmed and frankly didn't understand how important you are to the brass. We couldn't take the risk that something would happen and we wouldn't have the equipment available if we needed it. So we kept you here. They claim we cost some lives as a result."

"Cost some lives. What happened here?"

Marshall took a deep breath. "Yeah. So, this is where the necessary stress begins." He paused for a second. "There was an outbreak."

The man felt a cold chill. If the virus had made it onto the island, it was all lost. "How bad?" he asked, dreading the response.

"I lost almost half of my company," replied Marshall. The man understood the reason for the haunted look. "It broke out in the refugee camp. We followed doctrine and called in an air strike."

"Obviously not nuclear," the man interjected.

"No. Incendiary. My men kept the camp contained until the jets could get there. It didn't take long; there's a carrier parked out in the strait. Only a few of them survived."

"I'm sorry," said the man, feeling compassion for the officer.

Marshall was silent for a moment; the man could see he was lost in thought. Finally, he replied. "We all knew what we signed up for. Some of the boys are taking it pretty hard though."

The man understood the reason for the gentle way that the major treated the private who'd fetched his meal.

"You contained it. The outbreak."

"Yes."

"Any idea of the source?"

"St. John's thinks there may be a delayed onset of symptoms in some people. Two other camps on the island went at about the same time. They were contained as well."

So not, thank God, airborne, thought the man. Or carried by birds. At least that's what he was hearing here. He now found himself desperately wanting to talk to someone in the new labs.

"What can you tell me about conditions on the mainland?" asked the man.

"I can tell you what I've heard," replied Marshall. "Keep in mind that I'm just the local commander; I get told what I need to execute my orders and not a whole lot more. And like I said before, we're having communications issues. But there's a pretty active grapevine if you're interested in that."

"Go ahead. Remember, I know a lot less than you at this point."

"Okay. Here goes." Marshall took a deep breath. "So North America is officially quarantined. We're enforcing it along with a UN coalition. I think the quarantine was in place before you got here, so you already knew that. Right?"

"Yes," said the man.

"Aside from here, part of Labrador, part of Alaska and some other communities in the Arctic, it's a no-go zone. The virus was stopped at the Darien Gap, so it didn't make it to South America. And Europe and Asia and the rest of the world are clear as well. The big bunkers — Cheyenne Mountain, North Bay and a few others — are still operating. Oh, and some silos in the American mid-west. We can't get to them though. It's too hot."

It was better than he'd feared, thought the man, the Plan still had a chance.

"Speaking of hot," continued Marshall, "we used quite a few nukes towards the end to try to control things. There's been a fallout scare here and overseas, and the UN has warned us not to use any more."

"How bad has the radiation been?" asked the man.

"It depends who you talk to, of course. For public consumption, not a big concern if some precautions are taken. Privately, there's some fear about the long-term repercussions. Cancer and birth defects."

The man nodded. It had come up during the planning. Another reason he'd been against it.

"The American government is officially operating out of Gander. Unofficially, word is that they may have some breakaways. Hawaii for one — they managed to keep it clean of infection — and Alaska has been making some noises as well. So far, their military is still following the orders from the group here, but St. John's is worried about it."

Lovely, thought the man, political ambition added onto this mess. He guessed he should have expected it, but the stupidity rankled him just the same.

"What about the infected? Has there been a die off?" This was something they'd been counting on back during the planning.

"I'm not sure — either officially or unofficially. I'm afraid you're going to have to find that out when you talk to St. John's."

Their discussion was interrupted by the private. The man caught a glimpse of the nurse from earlier in the day as the soldier entered.

"Excuse me, sir. They're here to move him. They said you okayed it, sir."

"Yes, that's fine Jimmy, I did. Go ahead and let them in." The soldier walked to the door and opened it, allowing the nurse and two orderlies to enter the room. The orderlies were pushing a gurney.

"I guess that's it for now," said Marshall, "I let St. John's know that you were conscious. They want to talk to you, but they're getting a briefing package put together for you first to get you up to speed. I'll come back when its ready."

"Thanks," replied the man. "And thanks for the food."

"You're welcome." Marshall shook the man's hand again. "Take good care of him," he said to the nurse as he left the room.

She hadn't heard any explosions for a while. It was hard to tell though; the ringing in her ears was painfully loud. She waited for the soldier on top of her to move. He'd know when it was safe.

Finally, she couldn't wait any longer. The pieces of gravel digging into her face were becoming unbearable. It had started to drizzle as well; she could feel water starting to seep into her clothes.

And something pointy was jabbing into her back.

"Is it over?" she asked, hoping that her voice was loud enough to penetrate the ringing she was sure the soldier also had in his own ears.

No response. She asked again, louder this time. Still nothing. Something was wrong, she thought.

She began to squirm, trying to get out from underneath the weight on top of her. There was no movement from the soldier in response. This is what they call dead weight, she thought, fearing the worst.

Eventually, she managed to inch out from underneath the body on top of her, and rolled away as soon as she was free. She saw the length of rebar impaling him. She stood shakily, looking for the other member of her escort. She saw him several feet away. His head was gone.

She climbed the embankment to the access road and stood in shock as she took in the destruction in front of her. Where the camp used to be was now a tract of blackened, cratered land. She could see small smoldering heaps scattered across it. A tumbled pile of scorched metal sheeting and beams were all that remained of the processing building. She noted with satisfaction that the hated ferry was burned to the waterline.

She raised her gaze and saw that the town itself looked untouched. Thank God, she thought, Joshua would be safe.

"Over there!" She heard a shout and saw a mix of civilian firefighters and troops. They were spread out, obviously looking for survivors. One of the soldiers started heading towards her, with two of the firefighters following him. She sunk to her knees, suddenly overwhelmed.

"Stand up!"

The men were closer to her now. She saw that the soldier had his rifle pointed at her, and the firemen were hanging back. They're not sure if I'm one of the infected, she thought, and slowly rose to her feet. She recognized the soldier.

"Say something! What's your name!" he demanded. He looked nervous. She could see his finger on the trigger.

The infected don't talk, she thought.

"You know very well what my name is," she replied, more calmly than she felt.

The soldier relaxed and lowered his rifle. Not all the way, she noticed. "She's okay," he said over his shoulder to the firefighters. One came forward to examine her. The other moved off to inspect the bodies of her late escort. She could see him look briefly at the headless one, and then crouch to check the pulse of the impaled one. He shook his head at the soldier, who was watching tensely.

"You're lucky," said the fireman with her, "some scrapes and bruises from what I can see. We'll get you to the hospital for a proper examination though."

An animal howl, and a short rattle of gunfire from the direction of the devastated camp. All three of the men jumped. "Jesus," one swore quietly. They watched as a line of troops walked slowly and in unison across the burnt landscape. Occasionally one would stop and inspect a body while others covered him with their rifles.

"How many survivors?" she asked.

"More than you'd expect," the fireman replied. "More infected too." Another brief rattle from the camp. This time they all jumped.

"Let's get her out of here," said the soldier, still transfixed by the scene below.

Mary sat waiting for a doctor to see her. There were others more seriously injured, the triage nurse had informed her tartly when she was brought to the hospital. Mary told her she felt fine; just a few cuts and scrapes. And the ringing in her ears had died down. The nurse insisted she wait anyway and took a blood sample and left. The soldier who had brought Mary in didn't leave until the nurse returned and nodded to him. Before he left she made him promise to let the woman who looked after Joshua know that she was all right.

As she waited in one of the hard chairs lining the wall, she watched the crowd of staff and patients milling around her. The triage nurse had been right, there were a lot of people more seriously injured than her. The burned soldiers were especially hard to look at. She couldn't help but think of her missing husband when she saw them.

The throng of victims gradually cleared, and the people who were left seemed to have less serious injuries, more like hers. She thought that if she wasn't able to see a doctor soon she'd just leave and treat herself when she got home. She was anxious to see Joshua.

She saw a gurney wheel past her and started in surprise when she realized who was lying on it. Their eyes met and he smiled slightly. She saw his head tilt back to address the orderly pushing his gurney, and they came to a halt. She rose and walked over to him.

"Hello, Mary," said the man.

CHAPTER FOUR

Orientation

The man sat upright in his hospital bed, reading. A thick manila envelope had arrived that morning, just as Harry said it would. It was marked with a distinctive red border and grave warnings stamped in large block letters on both sides. He would have been worried about opening it if his name hadn't been prominently printed on the front. It had arrived, he was told, from St. John's via the carrier out in the strait, which had then couriered it to the hospital by helicopter. The man thought the whole thing overkill until he broke the seal and started reading the contents.

He'd absently spread the documents and charts and photographs on both sides of him as he pulled one horror after another out of the bulky envelope. There were a lot of horrors.

As Harry had reported, there wasn't a lot of the old North America left. The man had expected this. The circumstances of the last safe zones, however, were grim. Grimmer than Harry knew, the man thought.

The most pressing problem was food. Before the evacuation, the government had diverted as many container ships to the island as they could. The general confusion in the media had prevented this from being noticed and commented on, but more people had ended up on the island than planned for and what they managed to divert wasn't enough. Overseas allies were nervous about sending anything — even aid — through the quarantine. The result, according to the projections, was that even with the tight rationing that was currently in force there was only a little under a month left until the crisis hit in full force. There was already unrest in the cities and bigger towns as a result of the existing rationing.

The far north was in better shape; the yearly supply runs having been completed before everything started breaking down. The same wasn't true for installations like North Bay, who were almost out of food and fuel. St. John's was working on a plan to resupply them in the middle of the hot zone. The man had doubts about this.

He read on.

NORAD was reporting that the Chinese and Russians were performing reconnaissance of North America; the Chinese along the West Coast from Vancouver down to Los Angeles, the Russians concentrating on the Arctic. So far, it looked like aerial reconnaissance only. Neither country had landed people. The man hoped that they were smart enough not to, but he resigned himself to the fact that they probably weren't. He hoped they'd have a vaccine ready before the two countries carried the virus home.

And of the virus itself, it looked like the researchers in the labs were still struggling with it. According to the enclosed brief, they were missing some vital information that hadn't made it to the new labs during the evacuation. The man recognized what they were looking for. It would be hard to get to now, but obtaining it would have to become the highest priority if they were to have any chance of the Plan succeeding.

There was no mention about the rumors of the American's problems with breakaways. Assuming the rumors were true, the man guessed that St. John's hadn't wanted to send such sensitive information by way of a US Navy ship.

The final briefing item he pulled out of the envelope was a shock. The problems he'd read about so far could and in some cases had been predicted and planned for. They were bad, but not insurmountable.

He stared at the fuzzy still frames from the fighter's gun cameras as his mind churned, trying to work out the implications of what he was seeing.

The pictures showed a group of people removing the contents of a transport truck. Maybe boxes of food. It looked orderly, and the man would have thought them to be survivors foraging for food if not for the subsequent gruesome frames from the video. There was no doubt that these weren't survivors.

They're cooperating, he thought. That shouldn't be possible.

The man consulted the attached notes. A week ago, over Winnipeg. The fighter's mission wasn't stated, but the man thought he knew what it might have been.

The man was still speculating about the photographs when there was a knock on the door. A moment later it opened a crack and a raven-haired head poked through.

"Feel like a visitor?" asked Mary.

The man hurriedly gathered the papers surrounding him and stuffed them back in the envelope.

"Sure," he replied, "come in, Mary."

The young woman entered the room and looked around it. Her eyes lingered on the conspicuous envelope for a moment before she turned her gaze to the man.

"How are you feeling?" she asked, "You look a lot better than you did yesterday in the hallway."

Truth be told, the man *was* feeling a lot better. He suspected this was partly due to the pain medication, but mostly because he was doing something that was occupying his mind. Even if it wasn't pleasant.

"I'm feeling quite a bit better," he replied, "how about you? You looked like you had a few injuries of your own yesterday." He saw that Mary sported a number of bandages, including several on her pretty face.

She smiled. "My injuries weren't very serious. It isn't like I was shot or anything."

The man smiled ruefully in acknowledgment.

"Thanks for getting that USB stick to Harry Marshall," he said, "and I guess I also have you to thank for getting me on the ferry."

She shook her head. "No, the soldiers did that once they found out who you were. I just came along for the ride." She chuckled. "They brought your motorcycle along too. They didn't know if there was anything important on it, so they just wheeled it on. I think it's still parked over at the college."

The man smiled back. He would be happy never to have seen that particular item ever again.

Mary's face turned serious. "They got the bastard that shot you, too."

Another casualty added to the millions, thought the man. He wondered what the shooter had hoped to accomplish. He guessed that it was simple fear and frustration that had turned into blind rage.

"Why don't you sit down, Mary," he said.

"Okay," she replied, pulling a chair over to the man's bedside and sitting down, "but I can't stay long. They have me helping out here in the hospital now that the camp's gone. There isn't a lot of work though."

"How's Joshua?" he asked.

"He's fine," she replied, "the woman who owns the house we're staying at looks after him during the day. He likes her, and she's good with him. Her own boy is grown up and lives on the mainland. Lived, I guess. I haven't asked too many questions, and she doesn't really talk about him."

"And your husband," said the man, "any word about him?"

"Only that he's supposed to be in Labrador," she replied, "Goose Bay. One of the town employees was trying to help me track him down. He said that the military wasn't sure exactly where his unit was."

Goose Bay, the man thought. Well, that made some sense. It was a big military base and was isolated enough that it'd be unlikely any of the infected would make it there. The few that did could be easily taken care of; that must be what Mary's husband's unit was there for.

She continued. "Tom — the town employee — he didn't make it out of the camp before, well, you know what happened there."

The man nodded. He did.

"I'll do what I can to find out where he is when I talk to St. John's," he said.

"Thanks," she replied, "I'd appreciate it."

Silence followed, and the man could see a hesitant look grow on Mary's face as she prepared to ask him something else. He waited.

"I wanted to ask…you always seem to know what's going on…how bad is it out there really? We don't get a lot of news." She was looking at the envelope as she asked this.

The man thought of telling her not to worry; that everything would be fine; that the world would soon be back to normal. But he only considered it for a moment before deciding on the truth.

"The island is pretty much safe. They think that the incidents with the refugee camps were isolated…"

"Camps? It wasn't just this one?"

"Two others. All of them were contained, so the virus isn't an issue. For now, anyway. There are always risks. And the fallout has mostly passed, so that isn't going to be a worry for much longer. If we can get around the food shortages, everyone should be safe here until we can get back to the mainland. But getting back to the mainland…it's a whole other world there now, Mary. It'll take years, probably decades, to get it back to how it was. We won't see it in our lifetimes."

The man watched her as she digested this.

Finally, she spoke. "I guess that's what I expected. Thanks." A pause. "I guess I'd better get back to work."

The man nodded, still watching to see how she was taking the revelation. "Okay. Well, I'll be here if you feel like dropping in for a visit again."

Mary gave him a bright smile as she stood up. "I will. I think Joshua would like to see you as well. Maybe I'll bring him along if the hospital is okay with it."

"That'd be nice."

"Okay, well, see you later then."

"Goodbye, Mary."

The man watched as she left, wondering if he'd told her too much.

Each morning brought a new envelope with new information, delivered by an unsmiling airman. The airman was always in a hurry, as if he couldn't stand being away from the familiarity and safety of the carrier for any longer than necessary. The man marveled at the cost of delivering the envelopes to him and wondered why St. John's felt they needed to brief him using paper. He found the answer the fourth morning.

The reconnaissance by the Chinese had increased, particularly in the area of Vancouver Island. The intelligence agencies — both their own and the American's — were predicting an imminent landing. They were also suspicious that the Chinese had hacked the network infrastructure on the island and had accessed information on the current state of the two governments — remaining military strength, supply and the state of the civilian population. Intelligence believed that they'd already stolen a large amount of data and were using it to their advantage. A footnote to the report indicated that they may have the Plan.

It would work for the Chinese as well as themselves, thought the man, as long as they had a vaccine. Intelligence reports estimated it was unlikely. The man thought that the invaders would be insane to try a landing without one, but he supposed they had a large enough supply of warm bodies to throw at the problem. Too large, in fact, which was the reason for coveting North America in the first place. Both North American governments were trying a diplomatic solution, having lost too many of their resources to fight a war, but the Chinese were ignoring this, claiming that the territory had been abandoned. They also warned that nuclear strikes would be returned in kind, and pointed out the fragile nature of the island enclave.

The Russians were taking a different tact.

According to the next report, they were cozying up to the Alaskan state government, offering aid that the

American federal government was unable to supply. Food and troops, basically. This was the first time a briefing item had alluded to the rumors Harry had mentioned.

Alaska was a long way away, thought the man. He could understand why they'd be willing to take the risk, knowing full well that some kind of payment would eventually be expected in return. The American government wasn't happy and was making threatening noises, which were being ignored. They hadn't yet realized how powerless they'd become, he thought.

The man looked at his watch and saw that it was about the time that Mary usually dropped in. He found himself looking forward to her visits. Yesterday she'd brought along Joshua, but they hadn't stayed long after he'd lost interest in the stark hospital room. The man didn't blame him; he'd lost interest quickly himself.

A knock on the door, and the man gathered his papers into the envelope.

"Come in," he said.

The door opened and Harry Marshall entered the room.

"Hello, Harry," the man said in surprise.

"Good morning," replied Marshall. He nodded at the envelope. "I see you're being kept up to date."

"I am," replied the man, "although part of me wishes I wasn't."

"Pretty grim, isn't it," said Marshall.

The man nodded slowly.

"St. John's has decided to start giving more information to their local commanders," continued Marshall, "I know exactly how you feel."

"What have they got you doing now that the camp is gone?" asked the man.

"Not a lot," replied Marshall, "I'm waiting for new orders. I'm expecting we'll be sent to Corner Brook. The riots, you know."

"You're not very happy about that," said the man with a questioning look, seeing the expression on Harry's face.

"No. We're not police. We're not trained for it. And none of us signed up to fight our fellow citizens. But we'll go where we're ordered to go."

The lights flickered. It wasn't the first time it'd happened in the past few days. The man mentioned it to Harry.

"Yeah. The grid's overloaded. And add to that that some idiots have decided that they don't like all the extra people on the island and have started taking things into their own hands. It was small scale irritating stuff at first, but they blew up a power substation yesterday. I'm not sure what they think they're going to accomplish with crap like that."

"They probably don't either," said the man, "but it needs to be brought under control fast. Everything's fragile enough without people deliberately sabotaging things. Jesus."

"Another reason I'm thinking my troops are going to be doing some police work. I'll know soon enough though."

Marshall changed the subject.

"So the reason I stopped by," he began, "St. John's wants you there by the end of the week. They've talked to your doctor, and he isn't happy about it, but he's agreed that you'll be well enough to travel if you're careful. I'm supposed to arrange for you to get there."

Finally, thought the man. He was sick of being stuck in a hospital room while so much was going on outside. He also wanted to get more information about the pictures he'd seen from over Winnipeg.

"That's great," he replied.

"I thought you might feel that way," said Marshall, "anyway, the day after tomorrow we're going to put you on a flight off that carrier. You're getting the real VIP treatment. Anyone else would be driving."

The man laughed. He didn't feel like a VIP. A flight would get him there faster though, so he wasn't about to complain.

They were interrupted by another knock on the door. A familiar face peeked into the room.

"Decent?" asked Mary.

"Yes," replied the man, "come on in."

Mary walked through the door and stopped.

"Oh. Hi Harry," she said on spotting Marshall, "I didn't expect to see you here."

"Hi Mary. How's Joshua? Didn't bring him with you today?"

"No, this really isn't a great place for a kid. He's back at home with Mrs. Andrews."

The familiarity between the two surprised the man. As if sensing his surprise, Marshall explained.

"Mary's been helping out a lot around here. We keep bumping into each other." He laughed. "She appears to trust me a bit more than the first time we met."

Mary smiled. "Yes, Harry seems to be all right. Were you two in the middle of something? I can come back later."

"No, that's fine. Harry was just telling me that I'll be going to St. John's in a couple of days."

"I know," replied Mary, "and I was thinking that maybe you'd like a real meal before you leave." The man saw that she was blushing slightly. "I mean, it's kind of the least I can do to thank you for...well, you know... everything."

"I'd like that. Thanks, Mary. But I thought there weren't many groceries left in town."

"It's a problem. I have some friends though, and you're such a celebrity and all. It won't be anything fancy, but probably better than what you've been getting here."

"I'm sure it'll be great," said the man.

"Okay, well, tomorrow night then," replied Mary, "say 6:30. And you're invited too, Harry."

"Why, thanks Mary," said Marshall with some surprise.

"See you both then." Mary turned and left.

There was silence between the two men for a moment.

"She's quite something," said Marshall.

The man nodded. "She is," he replied. He paused. "What's going to happen to her if you're reassigned?"

"She'll be fine; she's fitting in well in the town. She's not going to be any worse off than anyone else here. And I've already talked to the woman who owns the place where she lives, and to the town and hospital staff. They're all happy to have her." Marshall looked thoughtful for a moment. "It's funny that even with all the death and destruction how much we've become concerned about one person, isn't it."

Silence again as the men considered this.

"Well, I'd better be off," said Marshall finally, "I'll come and collect you tomorrow evening for dinner. I'm sure you're not going to want to walk."

"Thanks, Harry."

"See you tomorrow."

Marshall walked out of the room. The man continued to contemplate his last question for a moment before finally returning to his reading.

On the fifth morning, the man found himself preparing both for that night's dinner and the following morning's flight to St. John's. The envelope, delivered as usual, lay unopened on the table beside his bed. He'd look through it later. He didn't think anything could be too pressing given that he'd be there in person tomorrow.

Since Mary had mentioned that the soldiers had brought his motorcycle along on the ferry that fateful day, he'd asked Harry if someone could have a look to see if any of his belongings had made it too. He did have a few items of clothing in his pack, which might still be on the bike, and the clothes that he'd been wearing on arrival were pretty much ruined. The hospital had laundered them, but he thought that wearing a shirt with a bullet hole to Mary's dinner would be in bad taste.

Harry had sent one of his troops off to look for his pack and a triumphant soldier had dropped off the man's belongings last night.

He found the act of shaving comforting in its mundaneness.

Having dressed and made himself as presentable as he was going to be able, he thought he'd take a minute and see what news was in the envelope. It was thinner than usual. He sat in one of the room's chairs and tore open the flap.

The man had already read about some of the missions that had been undertaken over the past few weeks. There were reactors that had needed to be shut down safely, equipment left behind in the evacuation that was now needed and general reconnaissance. The government desperately needed to know the state of the infection and the infected. Small teams were used; it was the only way to make it in and out quietly. And the survival rate was still appallingly low.

The mission the man was reading about now had been to investigate the scene caught in the pictures he'd looked at that first morning. St. John's was as concerned as he'd been. Without a die off, which according to the document didn't seem to be happening at the scale they'd expected, the Plan could be unworkable.

The team's radio reports had confirmed an unexpected number of the infected still surviving and, seemingly, thriving. While they didn't witness anything like what had been captured by the fighter's cameras, they did report seeing the infected in groups and acting in a shockingly peaceful manner towards one another.

But not towards the team. North Bay, which was coordinating the mission, had lost contact with them suddenly. Attempts to reestablish communications had failed, and a search plane had been dispatched from Goose Bay to investigate. They'd searched for as long as they could, attempting to raise the team by radio, but received no response and saw no sign of them. They hadn't dared to land. St. John's had officially written the team off, the loss of such expeditions having become almost routine.

The man finished reading the report and sat quietly, formulating theories about the behavior of the infected. Absently, he skimmed through the list of the dead and missing.

And recognized the name of Mary's husband.

CHAPTER FIVE

Last Meal

Harry arrived early to pick up the man for Mary's dinner. He wore his usual combat dress.

"I'm afraid I don't have anything more formal than this with me," said Harry. He looked embarrassed.

"It's fine," replied the man, "I don't think anyone will care."

Harry made a noncommittal noise, unconvinced. "Ready?" he asked.

The man handed Harry the report.

"Are you sure I'm cleared for this?" asked Harry, accepting the papers.

"I'm clearing you. Arrest me," replied the man.

Harry skimmed the report, his eyebrows rising as he hit the section on the infected's unexpected behavior.

"The last page," said the man.

Harry reluctantly flipped to the last page and read. "Damn."

"We have to tell her," said the man.

"He's listed as missing, not dead," observed Harry.

"Harry. What do you think the chances are that he's still alive? And if he is still alive, that he's still the same man and not one of those?" The man gestured at the pictures.

"You want to tell her tonight? She's going to a lot of effort for you. Do you really want to spoil it? She's waited this long to find out something about him, another day's not going to hurt."

The man thought about it.

"I leave tomorrow," he said finally, "and I'd like to be the one to tell her."

"When? Tomorrow morning just before you get on a helicopter? Let me do it."

"No. It's my responsibility."

"It's not your responsibility," replied Harry, "if it wasn't for you, she and her son would be dead or worse. You've already done far more for her than anyone else would have. Leave this to me."

The man considered the options while Harry watched him, waiting. Finally, he came to a decision.

"I'm telling her tomorrow morning. I'd appreciate it if you'd get on the line with St. John's and delay my flight."

"They're not going to like that," said Harry, "what do you expect me to tell them?"

"Tell them whatever you need to. Tell them the truth, in fact."

"Fine," replied Harry, "I hope you know what you're doing." He looked at his watch. "We need to be at Mary's in an hour. I'd better go and take care of this now."

"Thanks, Harry," said the man.

Harry grunted in acknowledgment. "I'll be back in a little while."

Harry left, and the man sat down to contemplate the evening.

"Your flight's delayed until tomorrow afternoon," Harry had told the man when he'd arrived. After that the two rode together in silence, both of them dreading the charade they'd have to play that evening.

The drive was short; the town wasn't that big, and they were the only vehicle on the road. Before they knew it, they'd arrived at the house where Mary and Joshua were living.

Mary opened the door and came outside as they were getting out of the olive drab pickup truck Harry had borrowed. It was clear that she was excited about the evening. Fairly bubbling, mused the man.

"You're right on time," she said, "come on in."

Harry and the man followed Mary into the house, Harry removing his beret as he did so. The smell of cooking filled the home. Seafood of some sort, thought the man, which made sense given the circumstances.

Mary led them into the cluttered but homey living room. An older woman was seated on a worn couch. Joshua was on the floor near her, absorbed in the contents of a cardboard box which were strewn around him. Toys that used to belong to the woman's son, the man decided. The boy looked up briefly as they entered, then returned his attention to the toys.

"This is Mrs. Andrews," said Mary.

"Mary's told me all about you," said Mrs. Andrews. "It's nice to finally put a face to the name."

"I hope it was all good," the man replied, recognizing the tired cliché he was using as he said it. He was distracted by Joshua.

"I think you already know Major Marshall," Mary continued.

"I do," replied Mrs. Andrews. "It's nice to see you again, Major."

Harry nodded. "And you, ma'am."

"Well, why don't you have a seat," said Mary, pointing towards a pair of empty, stuffed armchairs. "Do either of you want a drink before dinner? How about you, Mrs. Andrews, can I get you anything?"

Harry and the man looked at each other. Both could use a drink.

Mrs. Andrews spoke first. "No, I don't need anything, dear. I should probably come and help you anyway." She rose from the couch. "Why don't we get these fine gentlemen a glass of whiskey though. They look like they could use it."

The older woman knew something was up, even though Mary didn't, thought the man. "I'd love one, Mary, and I'm sure Harry would too," he said.

"Okay, two whiskey's coming up then. You don't mind keeping an eye on Joshua, do you?"

"No, of course not," replied the man, "he seems to be keeping himself pretty busy."

Mary laughed. "Yes, he is. We're lucky Mrs. Andrews kept all those old toys. Okay, back in a minute."

Mary left the living room followed by Mrs. Andrews, who looked thoughtfully at the two men for a moment before she left.

"What have you got there, Joshua?" asked Harry after the women had left.

Joshua looked up and inspected the two men for a moment before replying.

"Army man," the boy stated matter-of-factly, gesturing at Harry with a chubby fist that clutched a green plastic army figure. Harry and the man looked at each other, not sure if the reference was to the toy or to Harry himself. Harry decided on the former.

"Yes, I see that," said Harry, "I used to have some of those myself when I was a boy."

"You army man," replied the boy, Harry having guessed wrong.

"Yes I am, Joshua."

"My daddy army man."

Silence from Harry. Yes, your daddy used to be, thought the man, but even if he was still alive he probably wouldn't be recognizable as your father, let alone human. He looked at Harry and saw similar thoughts reflected on his face. They were saved by Mrs. Andrews, returning to the living room with their drinks.

"Here you go," she said, handing them the whiskey tumblers. Harry and the man murmured thanks.

"Dinner won't be too long. You can use the bathroom down the hall to wash up once you've finished your drinks."

She turned to Joshua. "And let's get you washed up as well."

"Army man."

"Never mind the army man. Dinner is almost ready. Come on now."

The look on Mrs. Andrews' face discouraged Joshua from making any reply, although he showed no intention of cooperating.

"He's at that age," said the older woman, walking over and taking Joshua's hand. He reluctantly stood and Mrs. Andrews led him out of the room.

The men sipped their whiskey, both of them thinking the same thing but neither wanting to be the first to say it out loud. Finally, Harry spoke.

"I'd forgotten about the boy," he said as if admitting a failure.

"I had too," replied the man.

They finished their drinks and took turns washing up. The man had just returned from the bathroom when Mary entered.

"Dinner's ready," she said, "come on in."

The men rose and followed her. The house lacked a separate dining room but boasted a sizable kitchen that took its place. The large old wooden table was set as if for a holiday meal, complete with place mats, china and cutlery that contrasted with the surroundings and were clearly only brought out for special occasions. A pair of candles in the center completed the scene.

"You're sitting there," she said to the man, pointing to the far end of the table. "Harry, you're at the other end."

The men took their seats. Joshua had already been placed on the man's left, elevated to the level of the table by a pair of cushions. The boy looked solemn and studiously kept his hands away from the place setting in front of him. The man smiled to himself, thinking that Mrs. Andrews had probably administered a pre-dinner lecture about proper behavior when dining with grownups.

Mary and Mrs. Andrews bustled about the table, setting out the meal. Fish was prominent, as well as potatoes. This is how all of the island's residents would be eating soon if they weren't already, thought the man.

Bowls and platters were passed around and plates were filled. He accepted the platter of fish from Mrs. Andrews on his right.

He hated fish.

He took three pieces.

Mary took care of Joshua's plate. From the boy's expression, the man thought that he wasn't happy about the fish either.

"Oh! I forgot," exclaimed Mary as the group was about to eat, "we have wine!"

She pushed back her chair and walked to the counter, retrieving the forgotten bottle along with a corkscrew. She brought it to the man.

"Would you open it?" she asked, "I always manage to break the cork."

The man stood, taking the bottle and corkscrew from Mary.

"Have a seat," he said, "I'll take care of it."

Mary returned to her chair. He was the center of attention as he carefully worked the implement into the cork. It felt dry. He wondered idly where Mary had managed to get it.

After a couple of touch-and-go moments, the cork was out in one piece. The adults smiled and clapped, and the man filled each of their glasses before placing the bottle in the middle of the table and taking his seat.

"This event deserves a toast," said Harry, taking his glass and lifting it.

"It does!" agreed Mary. Mrs. Andrews nodded and the man simply waited to see what Harry had in mind. He was afraid he might be the subject of it. He hoped he wasn't.

"To our wonderful hostess for preparing this fine meal," began Harry. Seeing Mary's warning look, he continued quickly. "And to our incredible good fortune at finding ourselves healthy and safe tonight when so very many aren't. Cheers!"

The adults replied in kind, stretching to clink glasses. The man tapped his against the plastic cup that Joshua held up hopefully, the boy not understanding the ritual but still wanting to participate in it. The man took a sip of his wine and set the glass down.

Polite conversation began slowly as the adults started to eat. They found themselves consciously avoiding the obvious topics in favor of trivia, in an effort to maintain the illusion of normality.

The man picked at his meal and noticed Mary watching him. He made an effort to appear more enthusiastic; dislike of fish aside, his disinterest had nothing to do with the food and everything to do with the grief he knew he was going to inflict on her.

The adults gradually grew more comfortable with each other as the evening progressed.

"Are you married, Major?" asked Mrs. Andrews.

"No, I'm afraid I never found the time," replied Harry, "I guess, as they say, I've ended up being married to my career."

"That's too bad. I'm sure you'd have made a good husband for some lucky woman."

Harry grunted.

"It's never too late, you know," she continued, "I met my own husband a little later in life. He was a military man like you."

Harry squirmed a bit, clearly uncomfortable with the direction the conversation was taking.

"I often wonder what he'd think of this mess if he was still alive," she said, more to herself than to the others at the table.

"Do you have children, Mrs. Andrews?" asked Harry. Mary and the man glanced at each other. Harry didn't know about Mrs. Andrews' son.

She paused for a moment before replying.

"A son. Grown up, of course. He works in Halifax. I haven't heard from him since this all started."

"He could be all right," Harry offered, "we know there are groups of survivors. People who managed to find a place to hole up."

She nodded. "That's what I hope for. I pray for him every day."

The man was impressed with both her and Harry's positive attitudes. It was even possible, he thought. The population density in that province was low enough that a careful group could avoid contact with the infected, if they chose the right place to take shelter.

"And how about you," asked Mary, turning to face the man, "is there someone in your life?"

His face must have reflected the pang of grief he suddenly felt. He could see that Mary was regretting having asked the question. He didn't answer for a long time.

"There was," he replied slowly. They waited.

"She's gone now," he continued.

The man could see that they didn't know what to say. He hadn't told anyone else and he avoided thinking about it. Maybe it would do some good to talk to other people.

"She was in Toronto."

Realization dawned on Mary's face. She was remembering the flashes on the horizon that first night, thought the man.

"Lots of people were evacuated from Toronto," Harry proffered, "There's a chance she got out."

"I watched her turn," said the man flatly.

Harry was silent.

"I'm so sorry," said Mary.

The man didn't reply, lost in his own thoughts.

They were interrupted by a knock on the front door. It was a welcome interruption.

"Now who could that be," said Mrs. Andrews, rising to answer the door.

They waited, wondering themselves who would be visiting. No one really visited for pleasure any more. Mrs. Andrews returned quickly.

"Major," she said to Harry, "it's for you. One of your men."

This won't be good, thought the man as Harry left. He could see the apprehension on Mary's face as well. They heard Harry talking to the soldier at the door but couldn't make out the words. Mrs. Andrews had sat down again but said nothing.

Harry strode into the room with the soldier in tow. Gone was the relaxed, affable man they'd just shared dinner with, replaced by a crisp military commander. He spoke in a clipped tone as he addressed the man.

"Orders from St. John's. You're leaving tonight."

"I thought it was all arranged for tomorrow."

"Change of plans. There's a helicopter waiting for you. You need to leave now."

The man made to protest. Harry bent over and whispered in his ear while Mary and Mrs. Andrews watched with concern. The man nodded and rose.

"It looks like I need to go," he said to them, "thanks for the dinner and the company."

He paused, considering whether or not to do it. It would be his last chance. Harry, watching him, shook his head. The man ignored him. He looked at Mary.

"Mary, can I have a word with you before I leave?"

The man sat alone on one of the protocol passenger benches along either side of the otherwise empty, windowless cargo plane, waiting for launch. A Greyhound, the crewman had called the stubby prop plane. He wondered whether it was named after the bus or the dog. From the look of the plane he didn't think it was the dog.

"*We're next for launch, sir*," he heard the pilot's voice say in his headset, "*make sure you're strapped in good and tight*." He acknowledged the pilot using the mic attached to the headset.

Mary had accepted the news of her husband surprisingly well, thought the man. He suspected she'd been preparing herself for it for some time. Still, he'd seen the pain in her eyes and had found it extremely difficult to leave after having broken the news to her.

He thought Mrs. Andrews would be a help in comforting Mary. She'd expected something like this from his and Harry's demeanor that evening, she'd told him quietly before he left. The man was also happy that Harry would still be around — for a while longer, at least — if Mary needed him.

He felt the strained tug of resistance against the catapult restraining cable as the engines revved to full throttle and tensed himself for the catapult to be engaged. The carrier's deck had looked awfully short to him as he'd been whisked across the flight deck from the helicopter to the cargo plane.

Suddenly, the man was jerked sideways toward the rear of the plane against the resistance of the crossed shoulder straps as the plane was hurtled down the flight deck. He understood the reason for the helmet the crewman had insisted he wear as his head scraped over a bulkhead brace. Moments later he was surprised to be subjected to a slight sagging dip down toward the ocean as the plane broke free of the catapult. Happily, he then felt it begin to gradually gain altitude and climb steadily.

Launch completed successfully, the pilot came back on the headset. *"Our flight time's about an hour, sir. It should be a smooth flight, so you can sit back and relax if you like."*

The man thanked the pilot and forced the tension out of his body, sitting back to contemplate what lay ahead for him in St. John's. Harry had been discreet in telling him the reason he'd needed to leave right away, and those he'd met since leaving the house obviously didn't know. They would soon enough though.

The virus was loose in the world.

CHAPTER SIX

St. John's

The man felt the plane touch down in a surprisingly gentle landing. He wished he could have seen the city as they'd approached it, but the windowless Greyhound had prevented it.

The plane began to taxi and the pilot advised him that they'd be at the terminal in a couple of minutes; there was no other traffic ahead of them. The man found that statement faintly disquieting, even though it wasn't surprising.

Before he knew it, the plane came to a stop and the engines shut down. The man waited a moment to make sure they'd arrived, then unbuckled himself and removed the helmet and headset. He heard activity at the rear of the plane and the sound of the ramp beginning to open. He rose and walked towards it to wait.

The ramp finished opening and the man could see that dusk had fallen. A soldier peered into the interior of the aircraft and spotted the man.

"Evening, sir," said the soldier, "hope you had a good flight. If you could follow me, there's a car waiting for you."

The man walked down the ramp and looked around. There were far fewer lights than one would expect at a major airport. The "St. John's" sign on the top of the terminal building was dark. He could see litter caught in the uncut grass off the tarmac and small drifts of it piled against some of the buildings. Dark windowed jetliners filled all of the slots at the terminal building. In the dying light, he could see more of them parked in the distance. Remnants of the evacuation, the man surmised.

What he noticed most though, was the unnatural silence. There were none of the normal sounds he instinctively expected: no jet engines, no cars, no voices. It felt abandoned, he thought.

"Any luggage, sir?" asked the soldier, jolting the man out of his thoughts.

"No," he replied, "I seem to be traveling a bit light."

"Okay, sir, could you follow me then please? They're anxious to see you."

The man nodded. "Lead on," he said, and gestured with an outstretched arm.

The soldier turned and walked in the direction of a gate in the fence past the terminal building. The man followed him, still distracted by the vaguely disturbing scene of the deserted airport.

It was apparent what vehicle was theirs; it was the only one in evidence as far as the eye could see.

Another soldier stood beside the idling black SUV, taking the opportunity to smoke a cigarette while he waited. He tossed the butt on the ground when he saw them approach. The soldier looked tense, his now-free hand close to his sidearm, looking ready to draw if things weren't as they appeared. Conditions must be even worse than he'd been led to believe, thought the man.

His escort nodded to the other soldier, who relaxed visibly in response and got into the driver's side of the vehicle. They reached the SUV and his escort opened a back passenger door.

"Please have a seat, sir. We'll have you to Government House in no time."

The man, about to get into the vehicle, stopped.

"Government House? I was expecting the University."

The soldier shook his head. "No, sir, our orders are to get you to Government House as quickly as possible. I don't know anything about the University." He paused, then added helpfully: "You can ask them about it when you get there, sir."

Orders are orders, thought the man, no use arguing. The brass probably wanted to debrief him first before he got to work in the labs. And anyway, he was starting to get a spooky feeling from the deserted airport.

"Government House it is then," said the man, and got into the back seat. The soldier shut the man's door, walked around the front of the vehicle and got into the front passenger seat. He closed his door and let out a barely audible sigh. "Let's get out of here," he said to the other soldier, who started the SUV and began to drive out of the airport parking lot.

The SUV sped through the deserted streets, the failing light making it difficult for the man to get a good look at the city as they passed through it. He remarked on the lack of people and vehicles. This was, after all, a mid-sized city, not a small town like the one he'd just come from. And it wasn't late enough yet for a curfew to be in effect.

"People are nervous," said the soldier from the passenger seat. The driver, focused on the road, grunted his acknowledgment. "Not a lot of fuel to spare either," the soldier continued.

"Nervous about what," asked the man, "the virus?"

The soldier took a moment to respond. He half turned in his seat to better talk to the man.

"Well, that's part of it. But the food shortages and the gangs are the real problem. Lots more people in St. John's than there were a couple of months ago. Not all of them the nicest characters, if you know what I mean."

"Gangs. Here in the city." The man knew about the unrest from the reports he'd read and what little information Harry had been able to pass on. He'd expected angry crowds though. Maybe riots. Somehow, he hadn't expected organized criminal groups here in the seat of government.

"Yeah. Actual gangs. Fairly well armed, too. The RNC was overwhelmed pretty quickly and the government asked the military for help. We're working with the RNC now to keep things together."

It took the man a second to place the acronym. Royal Newfoundland Constabulary, he remembered.

"I understand from a friend that you guys don't like police work very much," said the man.

"No," replied the soldier. "But if we didn't do it it'd all come apart even faster."

They were interrupted by the driver.

"Something up ahead in the road."

The soldier the man had been talking to turned back in his seat to look out the windshield. The man stretched to try to look out of it as well, but couldn't discern anything out of the ordinary.

"Looks like a roadblock," said the driver. The man felt the SUV decelerate.

"Wasn't there when we came through earlier," the other soldier replied and squinted, trying to make out detail as they approached. "Not one of ours, and not RNC. Pull over before we get any closer; we'll call it in."

The driver pulled the SUV over to the curb and stopped. The man could now see a roadblock consisting of a pair of cars parked across the road, their noses touching. He could make out a number of men standing at the blockade, but the encroaching twilight prevented him seeing much detail.

While the driver watched the scene in front of them intently, the other soldier used the car's radio to report the blockade. The voice at the other end promised to have a patrol to them in a few minutes. One was already close by, it said. It also told them to stay in the vehicle.

"It's armored," explained the soldier.

"Who are they?" asked the man.

"Remember those gangs we were talking about?" replied the soldier. "They've been doing this a lot lately. Trying for gas or food or whatever they can. Pretty easy for them to set up quickly, see what they can nab, and take off fast when the cops come. Or our guys. I'm hoping for our guys. They have more firepower."

"Here they come," said the driver, still watching the men at the roadblock, "they saw us pull over, I guess they got tired of waiting for us."

The man could see the silhouettes begin to walk towards them. As they got closer, the unmistakable shapes of rifles became visible. The man could see the two soldiers shifting in their seats and drawing their sidearms. There was silence in the vehicle as the men waited tensely.

"If someone doesn't get here soon, we run the barricade," said one of the soldiers.

"Agreed," said the other.

The faint sound of a siren could suddenly be heard, increasing in volume. The approaching figures heard it too — the man saw them stop, turn and begin walking back to the roadblock.

"Just in the nick of time," muttered the driver. The man could see the cars which had made up the roadblock part and drive off. They made a turn down a nearby side street and were lost to view.

Flashing lights were now visible, and a police car soon came into sight, slowing as it approached the SUV. The siren shut off as the car pulled alongside. The RNC officer driving the cruiser rolled down his window, and their own driver did the same.

"I take it we scared them off," said the officer.

"Yeah," replied the soldier, "they didn't seem as serious as the ones last week. Good thing, too. There were more of them than there are of us."

"It won't be long before they start to realize that. I'm not looking forward to that day."

The soldier grunted in agreement. "Anyway," continued the cop, "we're supposed to escort you the rest of the way. Why don't we get a move on."

"Good idea," replied the soldier. The two rolled up their windows and the police car performed a wide U-turn, placing it in front of the SUV. It paused for a minute and their own driver put the SUV in gear. The police car began to drive off and they pulled away from the curb and followed it. They accelerated to a normal speed, continuing on their way to Government House.

It was full dark by the time they reached their destination. The man could see what looked like a park, surrounded by a high picket fence. The streetlights glinted off the rolls of razor wire laying along it.

"Here we are," said the driver as they came to a wide driveway blocked by a pair of police cruisers, a number of uniformed police in front of them. An armored personnel carrier sat off to the side behind them, a handful of troops near it. Their police escort pulled into the driveway, and the SUV followed it.

A police officer approached the escort car as it stopped. The man could see several others standing and watching both vehicles, cradling short rifles. The driver's side window rolled down and the officer bent to speak with the occupant. A moment later he straightened and motioned for the parked cruisers to be moved.

"Someone ran the checkpoint a few days ago," commented the soldier in the passenger seat, "so they keep it blocked."

Their escort began to drive down the roadway. The cop waved for them to move, and their driver followed it. The man turned to look out the rear window. He could see the cruisers being put back into place. They don't waste any time, he thought.

They followed the driveway until they came to the front of a stately building. Security was more low key here; men in suits stood by the door. They may have been dressed differently but they wore the same wary looks as the cops and soldiers.

The driver put the SUV in park and the other soldier got out and opened the man's door.

"I'll take you inside, sir," said the soldier as the man stepped out of the SUV.

"Thanks," said the man as he looked around. In normal times this would be a pretty place. Even in the darkness he could make out the trees and gardens surrounding the old building.

"This way, sir."

The man followed the soldier past the plain clothes cops and through the main entrance. Several hallways and a staircase later, they arrived at a closed door. The soldier knocked.

"Come in," was the almost immediate response from the other side. The soldier opened the door and the man followed him in. The soldier saluted.

"Here he is, ma'am."

The woman seated behind the wooden desk clearly was or had been military, thought the man, even though she was dressed in civilian clothing. He was pretty sure he recognized her from meetings before the evacuation; he thought she might belong to one of the security services. If she didn't, he mused, she probably should. Fiftyish with steely gray hair and a stern, no-nonsense look about her, she certainly fit the part.

"Thank you, Corporal," she said to the soldier, who saluted and left the room, closing the door behind him.

"Have a seat," she said to the man, gesturing to one of the wooden chairs in front of the desk. The man seated himself and waited.

"Would you like a drink?" she asked.

"No, thank you," replied the man, "why don't we get right down to business."

She looked at him hard for a moment. "You've had quite the ordeal getting here, haven't you."

"I have," replied the man, and waited.

She looked down and sighed. "I'm supposed to give you a full briefing." She paused and then looked up again. "Those packets you've been getting came from my office. We couldn't put everything in them, but you probably guessed that."

The man nodded.

"Right now," she continued, "everyone who's anyone is here in this building. The Prime Minister and the US President as well. They're all in a meeting. The big decisions are going to be made tonight."

"How widespread is the infection overseas?" asked the man, interrupting her.

She took a second before responding. He'd thrown off her train of thought on whatever speech she'd been about to give him.

"It's going through Asia like wildfire," she said. "Not so bad yet in the Middle East and Africa. It's just started to hit Europe. A week, two at the tops before it's all over." She paused. "The Royal Family's been evacuated," she added.

"Where do we stand on a vaccine?" asked the man, "I assumed I was here to help with it."

There was no reply. She seemed to be thinking. Maybe preparing herself.

Finally, a deep sigh. "We did it, you know."

"Did what?" asked the man with apprehension in his voice. He knew what she was going to say next; he'd suspected it on the trip here. He'd hoped he was wrong. But it was in the Plan; a contingency that he'd prayed would never be needed.

"We spread it to rest of the world," she replied.

The man closed his eyes and shook his head. "Jesus. You had to do it."

"I suppose it wasn't actually us," she continued, "the Americans did it when the Russians and Chinese started to get too aggressive. Level the playing field, they said. They didn't tell us until it was done."

The man had been mistaken in thinking the Americans were powerless, he thought. He'd simply never really expected that they'd take that action — in the Plan or not.

He sat for a long time under her watchful gaze without saying a word, his mind working through the reasoning behind the decision and the implications. He eventually reached the same conclusion that the decision makers had. He nodded, more to himself than to the watching woman.

"There wasn't a choice," he said.

"That's the conclusion we came to as well."

"And the chance that someone's going to figure out who did it?" the man asked.

She shrugged. "It's possible. We do have suspicions that the Chinese have the Plan. The hope is that even if they do suspect us, they'll have bigger things to worry about. Retaliation is always possible though; assets are being dispersed." She continued to watch him thoughtfully, measuring his reaction to the information she'd just revealed.

"There's more, isn't there?" he asked.

She nodded. "You'll find this somewhat better news though, I think."

The man waited.

"We have a vaccine. A prototype, anyway, but it looks good. Your data contained the missing piece."

The man's eyebrows raised in surprise. "From what I read in your briefings, I thought..."

"Spreading the infection wouldn't have done any good if we spread a vaccine as well, would it?"

"No," agreed the man, "I guess it wouldn't have. You're not sharing it, are you."

She shook her head. "The only people who know about it, aside from the ones in the labs, are in this building."

"We're going to let billions of people die. Allow countless societies to collapse."

She sighed. "It hasn't exactly been an easy choice. What should we do? Let the Chinese take over? Or maybe the Russians? Or for that matter anyone else with a big enough army who's looking for more real estate. Aside from the nukes, the Americans are a third-rate power now at best. I can't imagine how far down the list we are. We could have easily ended up being bottled up on this miserable island for the rest of our lives. Which, by the way, won't be too much longer at the rate things are going."

The man thought for moment. "Still, there must be some way..."

She cut him off. "There's no choice and there's no other way. You know it and I know it. The virus needs to run its course overseas the same way it did here."

The man did know it, but knowing it intellectually didn't lessen the horror at what those countless masses of people were now or would soon be going through.

"We'll help the survivors," said the man. A statement, not a question.

She nodded. "Yes, we will."

The man took a deep breath and blew it out between his lips.

"What's done is done," he said finally, "and history will judge us all for it."

There was silence in the office as the man contemplated the enormity of what they'd done, and the woman watched him. Finally, he spoke.

"So given all this, my question is: what do you need me here for? You have a vaccine, you have the Plan. What was the urgency in getting me here?"

The man thought she looked relieved. She must have been afraid of a different reaction from him, he guessed. He personally found the situation sickening — he'd lived through, very personally, what was now happening overseas — but he'd also been one of the original drafters of the Plan. He had all the same information as the people who'd made the terrible decision and, he knew, he would have made the same one if he'd been in their place.

She began to answer his question when the phone on her desk rang. It was unnaturally loud in the quiet office and startled both of them. She picked it up.

"Yes?" she said tersely into the phone. She listened for a moment and the man could see her demeanor change. Someone important, he thought, not an underling.

"Yes, he's here, sir."

"I understand, sir."

"Yes, sir, I'll tell him, sir. Goodbye, sir."

She hung up the phone and looked at the man.

"They're out of the meeting," she told him. He waited for whatever it was she was supposed to tell him.

"The Prime Minister is ready for you."

"In every meeting and discussion, your name keeps coming up," said the Prime Minister as he shook the man's hand. "I'm glad to finally meet you."

"Likewise, sir," replied the man.

"You were one of those who drafted the Plan," the PM continued, looking at him intently, "so I'm going to ask you — and I want a no BS answer: is it going to work?"

The man had an idea of the pressure the Prime Minister was under. He'd had a momentary glimpse of it on the PM's face when he'd entered the office. It had almost instantly been replaced with the emotionless mask of a statesman.

"Yes, sir," replied the man, "I expect it will."

"We're going ahead with it," said the PM, "we're out of time."

The man nodded. He'd guessed this already.

"I'd like you in the first landing."

The man was surprised, and he supposed his face must have shown it. The PM nodded and continued.

"You're the only one of the original drafters of the Plan who has first hand experience with the infected out in the world. The only one who's still alive, at least." The PM said the last sentence quietly, almost as an afterthought.

That didn't sound good, thought the man. Still, he was tired of being on the sidelines as the world went to hell. Maybe he could make a difference.

"I'll do it, sir," he replied.

"I thought you would," said the Prime Minister. "The bombing runs have started, and the expedition will be leaving tomorrow morning. HMCS *Charlottetown* is waiting for you in the harbor."

The PM shook his hand again. "Good luck," he said. "And thank you."

CHAPTER SEVEN

The Mainland

"Gas! Gas! Gas!" yelled the sergeant.

The man pulled forward the hood of the bulky NBC suit and affixed his mask, checking the seal and canister as he'd been taught. He'd lost count of how many times he'd gone through this as the team drilled for their arrival on the mainland.

"Better," observed the sergeant. As the only member of the team who had no previous training with the protective suits, the man found himself the recipient of most of the sergeant's attention. He was starting to find it tiring, especially since the civilian versions of the suit, which he did have experience with, weren't all that different. He guessed that the sergeant was under specific orders to keep him alive though, so he accepted the scrutiny and corrections without complaint or comment.

The man had only been on *Charlottetown* for a short time before joining the troops on the ferry that was being used for transport — long enough to meet the captain of the ship whose guns and missiles would be providing any supporting fire the troops might need when they landed. After visiting the frigate, he was of the opinion that the ferry made for a lot more comfortable voyage than the warship would have.

The troops were congregated on one of the car decks along with their vehicles and gear and the man had decided to join them rather than spend the voyage alone in one of the ferry's lounges. There was a sense of purpose amongst the soldiers, and it buoyed his spirits to be with them.

He'd been inoculated by a military doctor when he boarded the ferry as had, he was told, all of the other members of the expedition. The doctor knew little about the vaccine except that the inoculation of the company as well as the frigate's crew had almost completely depleted their stock of it. The man realized this meant there would be no additional ground support until more vaccine was produced; the expedition would be on its own except for the frigate's guns and air support out of Goose Bay and Stephenville.

He'd seen the jets in the times he'd gone topside for fresh air. There seemed to be a steady stream of them going back and forth as they saturated the landing site and vicinity with the gas. The man had been told of the foul up with it; how they'd ended up with more of the persistent type — VX — than the kind that would disperse quickly — GB, or sarin. It meant more time in the NBC suits than anyone would have liked, even though the VX would be used in the outlying areas rather than the ones that the troops would need to secure immediately. Both types would kill the infected though, and the man thought that the inconvenience of living in the suits was a small price to pay for that.

As he'd watched the jets he'd thought of the Americans currently conducting their own assault on the mainland. The two countries had parted ways at this point in the Plan, with the US deciding to secure Colorado Springs and then Denver. The man thought that they'd have a harder time of it than the group he was with, but he wished them well. He also hoped their departure would make St. John's and the other cities less of a target when retaliation for spreading the virus came. Assurances to the contrary aside, he was certain that it would.

The voyage to the mainland had been smooth so far, and if he hadn't known otherwise, the man wouldn't have been able to tell that he was in a ship on the ocean. He checked his watch. A few hours out, from his reckoning.

Having completed the last training exercise, the sergeant approached him.

"Looks like you've got the drill down, sir," he said to the man. "We should be landing soon. I have to go and meet with the major and then marshal the troops. You can go up top if you like."

"I'd rather stay here," replied the man.

The sergeant nodded. "That's fine, sir, but I'll ask you to stay out of the way while we get ready. Don't want any injuries, you know."

"I will, Sergeant. Thank you."

The sergeant nodded again and turned and strode off to start the preparations for the landing. The man looked around and spotted a likely out-of-the-way bulkhead where he could sit — or crouch, anyway — and watch. He found the soldiers with their confidence and precision strangely calming, and he wanted to enjoy the feeling while he could. He also still felt some occasional pain from his gunshot wound. Nothing serious, in his opinion, but he still thought it was a good idea not to overdo it.

The man had a chance to talk to the major in command of the expedition just before the ferry docked. He'd spoken to him briefly before the expedition left, but the preparations for getting underway had prevented any detailed discussions. Dawson was the major's name, and he approached the man when he spotted him crouched against the bulkhead.

"Ah, there you are," he said, "thought we should have a chat before we land and make sure you knew what to expect when we docked." He held out his hand and the man rose and shook it.

"I have a fair idea," replied the man, "but I wouldn't mind some details."

Dawson nodded. "Well, air recon is showing that the gas seems to have worked as we thought it would. We're expecting the landing area, and most of the town, in fact, to be clear of infected. The first order of business is going to be to secure the terminal and yard. We'll be using it as a base."

"Do we have any idea if the gas has dissipated?" asked the man.

"No, not yet," replied Dawson, "we'll be in suits until we're certain it's gone." The man nodded. He'd expected this. Dawson continued.

"I'd like you to stay on the ferry while we're securing the area. I don't expect it to take very long, and I'm not foreseeing problems, but St. John's has emphasized repeatedly to me that I'm not to let anything happen to you."

"That's fine," replied the man, although it really wasn't. He hoped he wasn't going to be tucked safely out of the way for the whole expedition. He had work to do and he wouldn't be much good to the people counting on him back on the island if he was stuck on the sidelines.

"Good," replied Dawson. "I'm also going to assign an escort to you. They'll come and find you before we dock." He paused. "I think that's it for now. Were there any questions you had for me?"

The man had quite a few questions, but none that he thought the major would be able to answer. He'd find what he needed to know soon enough once they'd landed. He shook his head. "No, I can't think of any at the moment, Major."

"Okay," replied Dawson, "we'll talk more later. See you on the mainland." He shook the man's hand again, turned, and left.

The cavernous car deck was filled with the roar of diesel engines and the smell of diesel exhaust as the convoy of armored personnel carriers and troop transports prepared to disembark. In the lead of the column was a large olive-drab bulldozer. The man thought that that had been especially good planning. He remembered back to the last time he was here and the crush of desperate people attempting to board the last ferry out. He was sure most of them hadn't made it, and it was unlikely that they'd have had the courtesy to tidily move their vehicles out of the way.

Armed troops in full battle gear and NBC suits stood in ranks at the rear of the column. The man thought they looked particularly serious, and there was no discussion in the ranks as the company waited for the ferry's doors to open on the unknown world ahead of them.

"The word is that we're not expecting any resistance," said one of the soldiers with him, his voice muffled by the mask of the suit that each of them wore. His escort had found him, as Major Dawson had said they would; there were two of them — Stevens and Nicholson. The man was surprised to see that Nicholson was a woman. It'd been hard to tell at first with the protective clothing covering her, but he'd realized it soon enough. He knew that the military had female combat troops, but for whatever reason he still found it hard to get used to. He supposed his age was showing.

"I guess we're going to find out in a minute, aren't we, Charlie," replied Nicholson, her voice equally muffled.

They heard the clanging of doors opening and ramps being lowered, followed by the sound of the diesels revving up. The column began to move out.

"And off they go," observed Stevens quietly.

"How long do we wait?" asked the man.

"They'll radio when the area's secure," replied Nicholson. "If they're right and all the infected are dead, it should be pretty quick. I hope so, anyway. I hate these suits."

The man wondered idly how she managed to relieve herself while wearing the suit. He guessed that however she had to do it, it was awkward. He'd have to remember to ask Harry. If he ever saw him again, that is.

"Why don't we wait topside," suggested Stevens, "there's no reason for us to hang around down here, and we can watch what's happening."

"Good idea," replied Nicholson. The man grunted his agreement as well. The three walked to one of the access doors and up several flights of stairs, Stevens in the lead. He seemed to know where he was going, and the other two followed.

Several corridors and hatches later, they emerged on a walkway. Stevens led them along it, and the man caught sight of *Charlottetown* sitting off in the distance. For some reason, he found its presence ominous rather than comforting.

Eventually the trio reached the bow of the ship. The man found he was sweating, even though he hadn't really exerted himself. The suit was more uncomfortable than he'd thought it would be. It was going to become a problem if they ended up having to spend a prolonged time in them in the late summer weather.

"Here we go," said Stevens, gesturing with his arm at the scene unfolding in front and below them.

The man could see the troops fanning out and taking up what he surmised were defensive positions, with the bulldozer pushing cars out of the way to make room for the military vehicles behind it. There was no sound of gunfire; the gas must have worked. Or the infected were somewhere else. The man wouldn't have expected them around the ferry terminal anyway — there was nothing here for them.

He watched as a squad entered the terminal building that was to be their command post. As the troops forced open the doors and passed through them the man's eyes were drawn to the remains at the sides of the entrance. Camouflage patterned rags covered them. Soldiers who were left behind in the evacuation and tried to defend the same building, thought the man. He hoped this group would have better luck.

"How effective is this vaccine, sir?" asked Stevens suddenly.

The man thought about it for a second. The honest answer, he mused, is that I don't know. The last thing he wanted to do though was undermine the confidence of the troops. An answer like that would spread like wildfire. He decided on a different one.

"It's been tested, and the folks in the labs are confident in it. We wouldn't be here otherwise, soldier."

But we would, thought the man as he spoke. We're out of time.

"Okay. Thanks, sir," replied Stevens, who by his expression didn't seem to be completely convinced.

They continued to watch in silence, sweating in their suits, for what seemed like forever before Nicholson's radio crackled.

"We're secure here. You can bring him to the terminal."

Nicholson acknowledged and turned to face the other two members of their trio. "You heard it. Let's get down there."

The man followed his escort through the wedged-open terminal doors, glancing down at the dead soldiers he'd seen earlier as he did so. Disposal of remains was going to have to be a priority, he thought. They might be immune to the virus, but there were other diseases that they still needed to worry about.

The inside of the building bore all the signs of the panic that had gripped the site during the last days; paper littered the floor and overturned chairs dotted the hallway that the group passed down. A vending machine had been pushed over and cans lay strewn around it. The man idly kicked one of them out of his way as he passed. He watched as it rolled over an ominous looking stain on the floor and ended its short journey against a heap of bloody clothing. He glanced at his escort who had been watching as well. Their faces looked pale behind the masks.

The trio followed the sound of voices and quickly arrived at a door marked AUTHORIZED PERSONNEL ONLY. They passed through it and found themselves in the terminal's administrative office. Major Dawson, the sergeant from earlier and several other soldiers occupied the room. The soldiers stood guard while Dawson and the sergeant leaned over a desk, examining papers in the bright light from the room's windows. All of their masks were off and the hoods of their protective suits were pushed back. The gas must have dissipated, thought the man.

As if reading his mind, Dawson looked up and, seeing them, stood straight, the sergeant doing the same a moment later. "The gas has cleared," he said, "you can go ahead and take off your masks."

The man and his escort removed their masks with relief and pushed the hoods of their suits back.

"The area's secure," said Dawson, "we haven't come across any fresh bodies, so we don't know first hand how effective the gas has been. No reason for any of the infected to hang around here, I guess."

The man nodded. It was as he'd expected.

"We've found the generator, and according to these," continued Dawson, gesturing to the papers on the desk, "there's a good supply of diesel fuel. Someone had the foresight to have the tanks topped up towards the end. It shouldn't take long to get the power up, and we won't have any problems fueling the vehicles."

"How long until we can get out into the town?" asked the man. There were questions that needed to be answered, that would affect how quickly they could begin moving people off the island and back to the mainland.

"The first step is establishing the perimeter, which is happening now. We'll be moving the supply trucks off the ferry after that and setting up the camp. By nightfall, we should be set up. Tomorrow, if everything goes smoothly, we'll be able to start running reconnaissance patrols into the town itself."

More waiting, thought the man. He was getting good at it.

"Anything I can do to help?" he asked, "I'm feeling a bit like a fifth wheel."

Dawson shook his head. "I'm afraid not — at least not at the moment," he replied, "it won't take long though."

"I guess I'll go and check in with St. John's then," said the man, "give them a report on things so far. Not that there's too much to tell them yet."

Dawson nodded. "Good idea," he said, "and when you get back we can start planning for tomorrow."

Camouflage patterned cargo trucks were beginning to roll off the ferry, belching black smoke from their vertical exhausts, as the man and his escort returned to it. The site now secured, the soldiers had turned their attention to establishing a base from which the first concerted exploration of the mainland could take place. The bulldozer had been busy; the man observed it pushing the remaining cars off the pier in order to make room for the encampment the soldiers would assemble.

The trio still wore their protective suits for the time being, as did the other troops around them. The instructions were to always have ready access to them in the event of pockets of gas, and it was simpler to wear them than to carry them. They were far less oppressive with the hoods down — to the male soldiers, anyway. The man still had no idea how Nicholson was managing.

They entered the ferry across the open ramp, carefully avoiding the vehicles moving in the opposite direction, and took the same route topside as they had earlier. This time, however, they made for the bridge, which was manned by the ferry's civilian crew. They were receiving outrageously high danger pay for their part in the operation, the man knew. The authorities hadn't balked at all at this; money was valueless anyway and the crew would find that out too late to complain about it.

"I need to get in contact with St. John's," the man told the captain when they entered the bridge. The captain nodded and directed one of the crew to take him to the radio. It was, conveniently, located in a corner of the bridge out of the way of the current occupants.

"I'll need some privacy," said the man.

"No problem, sir, I'll get you connected and then it's all yours," replied the young sailor. He sat down at the radio and then looked at the man. "Who do you need to talk to?" he asked.

The man told him, and then watched as the crewman went through the process of establishing contact. It didn't take long; she must have been waiting for him.

"All set, sir," said the crewman, who rose and passed the handset to him. "Give me a shout when you're done." The man took the handset from the crewman and sat down. The crewman walked away, leaving the man's escort standing nearby.

"Do you need us to leave too, sir?" asked Nicholson.

The man shook his head and lifted the handset to his head.

"We made it," he said, without preamble.

"*I gathered that,*" he heard the voice say. It sounded impatient. He wondered how long she'd been waiting to hear from him. "*What's the situation?*"

"Too early to tell," he replied, "no infected at the landing site. We're going to start patrols into the town tomorrow."

"*Fine. Keep me updated. We're getting reports that the Americans are having a bad time of it in Colorado.*"

"Bad time of it how?" he asked. The man felt a pang of concern. The gas should have worked. He glanced up at Nicholson and Stevens, who were watching, trying not to look as if they were listening to the conversation.

"*Not enough details yet. We're trying to find out more. Watch yourself tomorrow.*"

The man heard a click and he guessed the conversation was over. He waved at the crewman who'd set up the call and passed him the handset when he walked over.

"All done?" asked the crewman, "That was quick."

"Done for now," he replied, "Thanks." He rose and looked at his escort. "Let's go," he said.

The man left the bridge with the escort in tow; he knew the way now, and he suddenly felt that he needed to talk to Dawson quickly.

CHAPTER EIGHT

War

"That's what I just got from St. John's," said the man.

He'd found Major Dawson, still in the terminal building. The man's escort had been silent as they'd followed him. They'd heard what he'd heard, though they'd pretended not to.

The building was in the process of being cleaned up; he'd seen small crews of soldiers working industriously, the signs of the previous struggle in the facility gradually disappearing. He noticed that the vending machine was now upright, and the spilled cans had disappeared, along with the body near them. The stain on the floor still remained as a grim reminder of what had happened here not that long ago.

Outside, large green tents were being erected in the freshly cleared marshaling yard as the base was prepared. The troops doing the work had looked less tense than earlier, the man had observed. Looking beyond the encampment, he'd seen others standing guard at points along the yard's fence, and armored personnel carriers had been deployed at the gates. It had all looked well secured to him, but he'd seen other well secured posts in the past that hadn't survived. He hoped this time would be different.

"I just finished reporting in," replied Dawson, seated at a desk in the administrative office. The desk had been cleared of the papers previously covering it and was now bare except for a map. A map of the town, the man saw. There was writing on it and symbols he didn't recognize.

"They didn't say anything about Colorado when I talked to them," continued Dawson. He looked up at the man skeptically as he said it.

The same as before: give the local commanders only the information they needed. Or what the higher-ups thought they needed. The man decided it was going to be different this time.

"My sources are at the top," he said, "if they say the Americans are in trouble, then it's a fact."

"And exactly what kind of trouble?"

The man shook his head. "No more details than that. We need to be cautious until we find out more."

"I don't know how much more cautious we can be," replied Dawson with sarcasm in his voice, "there's a full combat-ready company sitting out there, in case you hadn't noticed."

"I don't either, Major," the man said firmly, "I'll leave that to you, but I thought you should know."

"Fine," replied Dawson with a grimace. He thought for a moment. "We'll post more guards along the fence, and I'll pass the word down to be extra vigilant. I don't know what else we can do without details, and I don't want to spook the troops. Keep this to yourself. Agreed?"

The man nodded. "Agreed."

Dawson looked hard at Stevens and Nicholson, standing behind the man.

"Same goes for you two."

"Yes, sir," they each replied.

Dawson looked at them for a moment longer, his stare emphasizing the seriousness of his orders. Finally he looked away, took a deep breath and let it out slowly.

"Let's talk about tomorrow then," he said.

The man nodded.

"Pull up a chair," said Dawson.

The man sat in the passenger seat of the four-door green pickup truck (a "Milverado", he'd heard one of the soldiers call it). Private Stevens had asked to do the driving, explaining that he sometimes got carsick riding in the back seat, and he definitely expected to this time, being stuck in his NBC suit which, he said, didn't smell great. Nicholson had rolled her eyes at this, but had agreed and now occupied the truck's rear bench. It was way roomier than the guys had it in the armored personnel carriers they were following, she pointed out.

The man had seen the inside of the carriers back at their base. Claustrophobia must not be a problem in the military, he'd thought at the time.

He'd had somewhat of an argument with Dawson yesterday over his role in the reconnaissance patrols. Dawson, predictably, had wanted the man to stay at the base until the troops had a better idea of what awaited the expedition outside the fence. The man had had a different idea and insisted on accompanying one of the units. It wasn't until he'd suggested getting St. John's on the line to make the decision that Dawson backed down. The man thought that he might have made an enemy in the major: Stevens and Nicholson had watched the exchange, and it wouldn't take long for word of it to make its way through the company. On the brighter side, the pair's estimation of him seemed to have gone up.

Dawson had grudgingly provided the utility vehicle they now rode in, insisting on it rather than having the trio ride in one of the APCs. He wanted the man out of the way of the troops if they needed to react, he'd explained. His final words to the man before they'd left was to stay out of the way.

The convoy wound its way slowly through the town's streets, making for its assigned section. They were using a grid that the military planners had prepared, each patrol responsible for a square of it. They were likely going to end up on foot pretty quickly, the man thought as he looked out the truck's window. Many of the streets were clogged with abandoned cars, and the expedition currently only had a single bulldozer. They'd clearly be needing more than one. At least they'd been lucky with the weather; a perfect late summer day, if you ignored the end of the world.

The man felt the truck slow, and looked out the front window. The brake lights of the APC in front of them had come on.

"Over there," said Stevens, taking a hand off the steering wheel and pointing off to the left.

The man saw what the convoy had slowed for.

The gas had worked, was his first thought. Nicholson echoed it out loud from the back seat as she craned her neck to see the knot of bodies on the side of the road.

"Sir, are those...?" asked Stevens.

"Yes," replied the man. He realized that many of the troops in the expedition, maybe most of them, had never seen infected close up. Few who'd had contact with them had lived to talk about it.

"They don't look like anything special," Stevens observed doubtfully.

"They aren't when they're dead," replied the man. He was distracted. The fact that it was a group was disquieting.

"Charlie, you'd better pick up the pace," said Nicholson. Having slowed down to rubberneck, the convoy was now accelerating back up to its previous speed, leaving them lagging behind. Stevens stepped on the gas.

"And when they're alive, sir?" asked Stevens after he'd brought them back to their place in the line. "The infected, I mean."

They're like us, thought the man, with everything that makes us human stripped away. And terribly, terribly vicious. Rabid dogs, except that maybe, unlike rabid dogs, they've retained some ability to reason.

"Let's hope you don't find out."

They saw more dead infected as they progressed into the town; singly, in pairs and in small groups. The small groups continued to worry the man. Finally, the vehicles in front of them came to a stop. Stevens braked, not sure if they'd arrived at their destination or not — Dawson had neglected to provide them with a map of their own.

When the rear hatch of the APC in front of them came down though, they knew they'd arrived. Stevens put the truck into PARK and switched off the engine. They watched the troops boil out of the APCs and assume defensive positions. From what he'd seen, the man didn't think they had much to worry about. Yet, anyway. He was still nervous from his call with St. John's. He'd contact them again when they were back at the base to see if there was any more news about the Americans.

A soldier marched purposefully to the truck and Stevens rolled down his window as he approached. A sergeant. The man was momentarily amused at how well he was starting to recognize military insignia.

The sergeant leaned in the open window. The man read his name tag: "GORDON".

"This is it," said the sergeant, surveying the inside of the truck, "the road is blocked ahead, so we're hoofing it from here." It was as the man had predicted earlier.

"I'd like you to follow behind us," the sergeant continued. "Sir," he said, addressing the man, "I understand you'd like to get a look at the infected?"

Not really, thought the man, their physiology hadn't changed enough to make their reaction to the sarin gas any different from an uninfected human. He was interested in something else.

"Yes," he replied. It was easier.

The sergeant nodded. "Good," he said, "the more we learn about these bastards the better. I'd ask though that you stay with us and with your escort." He nodded at Stevens and Nicholson. "Please don't wander off and don't get in front of us."

"I'll make sure I don't, Sergeant," replied the man, although he intended to do exactly what the NCO had asked him not to as soon as he saw the need.

"All right then, let's get this show on the road," said the sergeant, and turned and strode off back to his waiting men.

The man and his escort watched the sergeant as he prepared his troops for their patrol.

"We're going to wander off, aren't we, sir?" asked Stevens. Nicholson chuckled from the back seat.

The man smiled.

"I think you can count on it."

Nicholson, Stevens and the man hadn't quite wandered off — they could still see a couple of the patrols in the distance — but they hadn't followed the troops as closely as they'd been asked to.

The screams that erupted from Nicholson's radio were the first sign that something had gone wrong.

They'd been looking at a cluster of dead infected. There were four in the group, one man and three women. Their clothes were in tatters and they were filthy and unkempt, but they'd obviously been eating — there were no signs of starvation. Malnutrition, maybe. One of the females' faces was frozen in a snarl, and the man could see missing teeth, incongruous in a mouth that had clearly been the recipient of expensive dental work in the past. Scurvy, he guessed.

"Anyone!" yelled the radio over the screaming. "We need help urgently!"

They heard a calmer voice, asking for the location. The sergeant, it sounded like. There was no response.

A burst of gunfire. They looked around, trying to determine the direction. A second burst and they had it. It was close. Nicholson and Stevens unslung their rifles and looked at the man, silently asking his permission to respond.

"Move," he said, and followed them as they ran in the direction of the gunfire. As they raced down the street, the man wished he still had his old revolver.

They were the first on the scene. A small white frame house. The lawn, like those of all of the other homes, overgrown with weeds and wildflowers. A bloody soldier lay on it, propped on his elbow and clutching his rifle, his radio beside him. The door to the house was open wide.

Nicholson was first to the soldier.

"What's going on?" she asked urgently.

He looked at her blankly for a moment, and then seemed to focus.

"Live ones in there." He gestured with the barrel of his rifle at the door. "They got Bennett and Dean."

115

The man, slightly behind Nicholson and Stevens, saw the bite marks on the injured soldier. The first field test for the vaccine, he thought grimly.

As if on cue, a female infected charged through the open door, wild eyed, her hair a matted mess, blood covering her mouth and running down her chin. The man and his escort were frozen with shock upon seeing her.

She was pregnant.

Nicholson reacted first and cut her down with a burst from her rifle.

She turned to the wounded soldier. "How many more?" she asked.

"What?" he responded. He was going into shock, thought the man.

"Give me your first aid kit," the man said to Stevens. The soldier fished around in his gear, found it and handed it to him. The man knelt and examined the wounds. Nothing life threatening, was his diagnosis. Except maybe for the virus, but they wouldn't know that for hours yet. He used the kit's scissors to cut away the soldier's uniform from around the bites and doused the wounds with the antibiotic powder from the kit. He remembered the old adage about there being nothing dirtier than a human mouth. He guessed that still applied even if the owner of the mouth wasn't technically human any more.

"How many infected inside?" Nicholson asked again, louder this time and more urgently.

The soldier shook his head slowly. "I'm not sure," he replied, "two more? Maybe three. It happened fast.

They got Bennett before we even knew they were there, and then Dean, he..."

The man finished applying bandages to the wounds. It wasn't the neatest of jobs, but he thought it would do until a real medic could take over.

"What were you doing in the house?" Nicholson demanded, interrupting the soldier.

"The door was open, and there was a path through the grass that something had been using, and we thought we'd better have a look."

The man saw the beaten track as soon as the words were out of the soldier's mouth: he hadn't noticed it until then. A group had clearly been using this house for shelter. This was bad, he realized. If the infected were holed up in buildings that the gas didn't penetrate...maybe this is what was happening to the Americans.

Yelling from nearby. Soldiers ran into the yard, rifles ready and fear on their faces. They weren't expecting this, thought the man. The sergeant from earlier — Gordon, he remembered — was in the lead. The sergeant hid his fear better than the troops under him, but the man caught a flash of it in his eyes as he surveyed the scene.

"What's the situation?" the sergeant demanded. He was looking at the man as he asked, but it was Nicholson who answered.

"Two or three infected in the house, according to Cole, Sergeant." She gestured with her chin at the wounded soldier on the lawn. "We don't know how many of them are still alive. Bennett and Dean are still in there. We don't know their condition."

Gordon turned to the man. "I told you not to wander off."

"It's lucky we did, Sergeant," he replied, nodding towards the dead infected female at the house's front door. The sergeant began to say something else. His face was starting to turn red. The man cut him off. He had no patience for this.

"We're wasting time," he said in a level voice.

The sergeant stopped, paused for a moment and regained his composure. He nodded.

"You're right," he said. He turned to his troops who stood watching. "Jackson, see to Cole. The rest of you, let's get in there."

The man was the second last person into the house. Stevens followed him. He was grateful for his escort's attention to duty, especially given that he was still unarmed. That was going to change at the first opportunity.

The smell hit him first. It was an animal scent, overpowering; a combination of unwashed bodies, rotting food and feces. He thought of putting on his suit's mask but thought better of it — his vision would be hampered, and he didn't want to take the risk.

The troops moved cautiously in and out of doorways off the short hallway, checking rooms, their bodies showing the signs of their jumpiness and their fingers resting on the triggers of their rifles. The tension was thick as they reached the last door. It was ajar, and two soldiers entered it, one after the other.

A burst of gunfire, deafening in the enclosed space. Another burst immediately after. The man waited for a third.

"Clear!" he heard yelled instead, seconds later. He followed the rest of the troops into the room. A living room or family room or the like, he saw as he entered it. Couches and a big flat screen TV. And bodies.

Well, he thought, gorge rising in his stomach, at least we know what they've been eating.

There was silence in the room as the group stood stunned, looking at the carnage. He heard one of the soldiers retching.

"Jesus," said the sergeant quietly as he mopped his brow.

There were three infected laying on the floor between the couches and the television, their hands and mouths covered with blood. Bennett and Dean had been the center of their attention. He could see other…parts…laying in heaps in the corners of the room. He gave in to his heaving stomach. He wasn't the only one.

"Check them," the sergeant said to the man, pointing at the infected. The man nodded and moved to examine the bodies, Stevens and Nicholson moving with him, covering him with their rifles. The room was silent and he felt a rush of apprehension.

The reek of carrion was overpowering as he knelt over the first body.

"Gloves?" he asked, over his shoulder. The sound of rustling. Nicholson handed him the pair of latex gloves from her first aid kit.

He took hold of a wrist. Blood smeared his gloves as he turned the hand. He stared at it for a moment, realizing that it belonged to one of the unfortunate soldiers. "Dead," he pronounced after checking the pulse. He moved to the next infected. The same ritual. More blood on his gloves.

"Dead as well." Now the last one. He could feel his heart beating.

He checked for the pulse of the last infected.

A hand closed on his, clutching it tightly.

He pulled back, dragging the body with him. He heard a yell, then another one. A roar of gunfire, and a spray of blood hit him. The hand relaxed and he stood, shaking, his muscles aching as adrenalin coursed through his body. "Nice shooting, Christina," he heard faintly, as if from a distance.

"Dead as well, I'd say," observed the sergeant. He looked at the eviscerated soldiers who'd had the distinct misfortune of first entering the house.

"Let's get them out of here."

The man examined Cole, the surviving victim of the nest of infected, in the small hospital tent at the base. Nicholson and Stevens stood behind him. So far, so good, he thought. The young soldier showed no signs of the virus.

The bodies of the others who hadn't been so lucky rested in a corner of the tent in body bags, awaiting burial. There'd been some heated discussion on this, but there was no way to get them back to the island for proper interment, and no way to store them until there was a way. *Charlottetown* had categorically refused to take them on board.

A nearby graveyard, outside the fence, had been earmarked for the purpose. The man didn't think this was the last time it would be used.

"How's it look?" asked Cole nervously.

The man smiled at the young soldier. "I think you're going to be fine," he replied. "I'll check back on you later," he said, and left the tent. Dawson was waiting for him outside.

"How does he look?" asked the major, repeating the soldier's question.

"I think he's going to be fine," replied the man, repeating the answer. "No signs of the virus. I think the vaccine's a winner."

Dawson nodded. "Well, that's a break, anyway. Now what about these live infected? What happened to this Plan of yours?"

The patrol the man had been with hadn't been the only one to encounter them. The others had been luckier though.

"Why don't we find somewhere to sit down and discuss it," said the man. There were too many others around. No use creating alarm with his speculations. Although they weren't really speculations anymore.

"Fine," replied Dawson, "let's do that." He turned and walked towards the terminal building. The man followed him, along with his ever-present escort.

Dawson led them to the administrative office. A soldier was busily setting up a radio set. He looked up as they entered.

"All ready, sir," he said to the major.

"Good work, Poole," the major replied, "can you give us a few minutes, please?"

"Yes, sir." He straightened from his task and saluted, then left the room. Dawson closed the door behind him, looked at the man, and gestured to a chair beside a desk strewn with maps. The man sat in the chair and the major took a seat at the desk itself. Nicholson and Stevens remained standing near the door. They had to be getting tired of doing all that standing around, the man thought idly.

"Now," said the major. "The Plan. What's gone wrong?"

The man wasn't sure how much the major knew. If he had to guess, he'd say only the very basics — that had been the pattern so far. Success hinged on the commander in front of him though, and the basics weren't going to be enough.

He took in a deep breath and let it out.

"I'd better start at the beginning."

The man told the story of the early days of the outbreak, and the growing realization that there was a distinct possibility that the human race wouldn't survive. He spoke of the late nights organizing the doomed safe areas, arguing over the use of nuclear weapons to control the hot zones, and the final deliberate decision to abandon the mainland and the millions of people on it.

"We knew there was no hope," said the man. "The goal changed almost overnight from one of containment to simple survival — and reconquering, if I can use that term, when we had a vaccine."

Dawson had listened without expression. "And that's the point we're at now, correct?"

The man nodded. "Correct," he said. "The idea — the Plan — was to use gas to clear out the infected, and move people off the island and back here to resettle. Gradually expand the cleared territory. We believed the infected were no better than animals — worse, in fact. We expected massive starvation and when winter came, we thought most of them would die from exposure to the elements. The gas would just speed things up so we could get started."

The man shook his head slowly. "You have no idea how hard it was to move all that gas up from Kentucky."

Dawson waited. The man continued.

"The problem is that the infected are turning out to not be as damaged as we thought they were. They can think. They're surviving. And they aren't going to just die off. It changes everything."

A knock on the door interrupted the man. The major nodded at Nicholson, who opened it. The soldier from earlier — Poole — stood in the doorway.

"Message from *Charlottetown*, sir," he said, "St. John's is looking for him. They say it's urgent." The man felt a cold chill.

"Well, come in and get them on the line," replied Dawson, "you said you have this radio working, right?"

"Yes, sir," said Poole, who walked into the room and over to the radio. He sat down and switched it on and began to make contact. This radio didn't seem to have a handset, the man observed; whatever was said would be heard by everyone.

It was quick. "Yes, he's right here," Poole said to whoever was on the other end. He stood and looked at the man. "All yours, sir."

The man walked to the radio. He didn't sit down. He had a feeling this was going to be bad.

"Yes," he said, "I'm here."

"*I only have a few minutes,*" she said. "*Listen to me: the infected are slaughtering the Americans. They're smart.*"

"We've come to that conclusion as well," the man replied.

"*You have.*" She sounded surprised.

"*Okay. Good,*" she continued. A brief pause. "*I don't know what you're going to do about it, but whatever you do is up to you. You're in charge now. Dawson, are you there?*"

The major cleared his throat and spoke. "Yes, ma'am," he said, loud enough for the radio to pick it up.

"*You heard that? He's in charge. Charlottetown's getting the same orders.*"

"Yes, ma'am."

The cold chill hit the man again. "What's happening?" he asked.

A grim laugh.

"*They figured it out, just like you thought they would. NORAD's reported missiles coming in over the pole. We're confirmed as a target.*"

"Can't you evacuate?" asked the man, stunned by the news.

"*It's too late now. There were too many preparations we had to make. The Prime Minister did want me to ask you to try to save as many survivors as you could.*"

The man felt numb.

"*The team from the labs is in a helicopter on its way to you. With luck they'll be out of the blast zone in time. That was one of the preparations.*"

"*I think that's it. There's a group that's got together to pray. I thought about joining them, but I think I'm just going to sit and look out the window for a while. It really is beautiful here.*"

He tried to think of something to say, but words wouldn't come to him.

"*Good luck, my friend.*"

CHAPTER NINE

We're On Our Own

The room was brighter for a moment, and the radio went dead. There was an eerie silence, and in it they could hear a bell ringing faintly in the distance. *Charlottetown*, the man thought. They've gone to battle stations. Moments later they felt the rumble, and the man knew without any doubt that they were on their own.

They'd been stunned by the last words from St. John's, and the tremor jolted them out of it. Dawson leapt to his feet and rushed out the door, yelling "Stay in here!" over his shoulder as he left. He had over a hundred troops out there.

"Get me *Charlottetown*," he said to Poole, the radio operator.

"Yes, sir." He returned to the radio and sat down.

"Are we likely to be a target?" asked Nicholson.

"No," said the man, shaking his head, "she would have told us." He thought about it for a moment. "Probably."

126

"What about radiation, sir?" asked Stevens.

"We likely caught some from the blast," he replied, "a slightly higher dose for anyone outside. Shouldn't have been enough to worry about. And the prevailing winds blow east, so we won't get the fallout." The island itself wouldn't be so lucky, he thought.

Voices coming from the radio. "I have *Charlottetown*, sir," said Poole.

The man spent the next ten minutes in conversation with the frigate's captain. The officer sounded distracted. There was, after all, a war going on. A long distance, push-button war. Not really a war even. An act of vengeance.

The Americans had launched their own retaliatory strike as soon as NORAD detected the missiles rising out of Asia. Their warheads would hit cities already doomed by the virus. It was, the man thought, all rather pointless.

Goose Bay was gone, he was told, as well as St. John's. Gander had also been a target, even though the Americans were long gone from it.

"North Bay?" the man asked.

"*They took a near miss, but they're still operating,*" was the reply, "*we managed to make contact with them for a few minutes; they're trying to coordinate remaining assets.*"

They were deep enough underground, thought the man, that a near miss wouldn't knock them out. He remembered that they'd been running low on food and fuel and wondered if the plan to resupply them had worked. He started to ask when the captain changed subjects.

"*I received last minute orders just before we lost St. John's,*" he said. He relayed them to the man.

His final orders were stay with the expedition and defend it as well as he could. He couldn't, he told the man, do much against ballistic missiles if they came, but they were on full alert for any other threats. The man couldn't think of what those might be. The captain also put the frigate at the man's disposal — he'd received the same directive as Dawson as to who was now in charge.

He asked for instructions.

"Keep doing what you're doing for now," said the man, trying to sound more confident than he was feeling and having no idea what the proper military language was. "You and I and Dawson will need to meet. The major is off with the men now, as you'd expect. As soon as he's back we'll have to work out a plan." A plan, he thought, not a Plan. That was done and over. Now it was just survival.

"*Yes, sir,*" replied the captain. He signed off.

The man watched the helicopter land, in an area cleared for it near the terminal building. The troops not on guard duty at the fences looked busy moving equipment and supplies. Stevens and Nicholson had also been reassigned — temporarily, he was told. He wondered what Dawson had the soldiers doing. He'd find out shortly.

Dawson joined him as the helicopter's door opened and the single passenger — *Charlottetown*'s captain — emerged and hurried to them. He was bent forward and holding down his hat as the blast from the aircraft's spinning rotors buffeted him.

He shook both their hands when he reached them.

"This is quite the mess, isn't it," he said.

"It certainly is," replied the man.

The man heard the helicopter's engines revving up and saw it lift off for the short return flight to the frigate.

"He's in a hurry."

The captain followed the man's gaze. "The Sea King's primary role is sub-hunting. It needs to get back to it. Remember those other threats I mentioned?"

The man nodded. It wasn't something he'd considered, but he supposed they were sitting ducks for a submarine based attack.

"Let's get inside and get to work," he said.

They walked the short distance to the building and entered it, and the man quickly found himself in the administrative office once again. The office was empty and the three found themselves chairs.

The man took a deep breath and blew it out slowly.

"So," he said, to no one in particular, "what to do."

Dawson was the first to speak.

"I have the troops preparing for refugees. We have extra tents and some extra cots, and we'll send squads into town for more. We should easily be able to house a couple of hundred people inside the wire if we need to."

That was good thinking, thought the man, and it was giving the soldiers a mission. But getting survivors back on the island organized and across the strait was going to take time. And the man guessed that they'd overflow whatever could be set up for them here almost immediately. They'd need to secure the town itself.

"We're going to need to secure the town though," continued Dawson, reading the man's mind, "and someone's going to have to go back and start moving people across the strait." Dawson looked at *Charlottetown*'s captain as he said this.

The man nodded. And there was something else. Something that was critical with live infected in the area. Something else that they were now on their own for.

"Those people aren't going to be immune," he said, "we need to be able to produce the vaccine."

"St. John's said they'd evacuated the labs," offered Dawson, "when they get here, we should be able to set up production, shouldn't we?"

"If they get here," said the man. "They were flying just ahead of a nuclear blast. I assume we haven't heard anything from them?"

The frigate's captain shook his head. "No," he said, "but that could be for any number of reasons. Atmospherics are wonky at the moment — that's one possibility."

"So we hope for the best," said the man. "In the worst case, we use the blood of those who've already been inoculated. And in both cases, we'll need a facility — not to mention things like food and fuel — so we're back to needing to secure the town."

He sighed, and then looked at Dawson. "So, Major, shall we get started?"

Once more, the troops entered the town. This time, though, it wasn't simple reconnaissance: they had a pressing purpose and they had a good idea of what might be lurking out there, huddled in dark filthy nests anywhere the gas might not have penetrated.

The man rode with the convoy making its way to the hospital. It was larger than the other patrols which were tasked with performing door-to-door searches and clearing; knowing what they now knew, they were expecting the hospital to be particularly bad. But it was the key to being able to absorb refugees from the island. They'd need its facilities to produce a vaccine if the evacuees from the labs made it to them. If not, they'd need it for transfusions. Slower and less certain, but better than the alternative — swelling the ranks of the infected would doom them.

It had been almost 24 hours since the destruction of St. John's, and there was still no word from the evacuation helicopter. They'd agreed that morning that *Charlottetown* would send its Sea King out to begin a search, fears of enemy submarines being put aside by the higher priority facing them. It was now following what they guessed would be the other aircraft's flight plan, trying to make contact through the still muddied atmosphere and looking for some sign of it or its passage. The man was still hopeful; there were any number of reasons for its delay — not all of them as a result of its destruction.

The mood of the troops was grimmer than the last time the man had been with them. As if in response to the general spirit of the soldiers, the sky was overcast and gray, and it looked like it might start drizzling at any moment.

Like the last time, the man rode with Stevens and Nicholson in an olive drab pickup truck almost at the end of the convoy. They weren't the last ones this time — a garbage truck followed them. They needed to start worrying about disposing of bodies.

Stevens was once again in the driver's seat. The trio was prepared for trouble, and the man had acquired a sidearm before leaving the base: a modern black semi-automatic pistol, the same as the troops carried. Its weight was comforting in the holster on his hip. He still would have preferred his old revolver, though. Revolvers don't jam.

The man saw that they were approaching the hospital. The convoy slowed, and the sea of cars occupying the parking lots came into view. They'd expected this. Scared, sick people would have flocked here in the final days, hoping for help. But the man knew that there hadn't been any, and he expected they would encounter some of those people when they entered the building, in a vastly transformed state.

The convoy halted. The driver of the lead vehicle was deciding on the best way to approach the building. A minute or two went by, and they started up again, turning down the driveway leading to the hospital's emergency entrance. It was clear except for a pair of ambulances and a police car pulled off to the side. The man could see the remains of a body clothed in a tattered police uniform lying nearby.

The convoy stopped in front of the entrance. Stevens brought their own vehicle to a stop. They were far back from the entrance itself. There were a lot of vehicles.

The man, Stevens and Nicholson would be waiting where they were until the building was secure. The man had agreed to this with Dawson. The troops knew what to expect now, and there was little he'd be able to contribute to the operation until the hospital was clear.

"Anyone bring a deck of cards?" asked Stevens as they watched the troops stream into the building.

"Never mind cards, Charlie," chastised Nicholson from the back seat, "keep your eyes open."

The man was restless as well. "I think I'm going to wait outside," he said.

"We'll wait with you, sir," said Stevens.

"Whatever you like," said the man, and got out of the truck. He closed the door and stood looking at the hospital entrance. The hospital's lab would be small, he thought, but it should still do the job for them.

Stevens and Nicholson joined him, rifles slung. Stevens pulled out a cigarette and lighter. "Mind if I smoke, sir?" he asked.

"No," replied the man absently. "In fact, I'll take one of those if you don't mind."

"Sure, sir, no problem," replied Stevens, holding out the pack. The man took one and put it between his lips. Stevens lit it with a battered Zippo.

"Those things will kill you," said Nicholson, watching the pair.

"I never get tired of hearing that, Christina," replied Stevens, drawing in a lungful of smoke and blowing it out slowly. "I think dying of cancer is the least of our worries though," he added.

They stood and waited. In the distance, they heard the sound of jet engines, quickly increasing to a roar. A trio of fighters screamed overhead, the markings indicating that they were theirs. The lead plane waggled its wings as it passed overhead.

"I guess we're still in business," observed Stevens.

"Where are they from?" asked Nicholson. "And where are they going?"

The man shook his head. "Where are they from? Stephenville, probably. Or maybe they got out of Goose before it was hit. Where are they going? I don't know. Wherever they can land, I guess. There aren't many choices for them."

They watched the jets disappear into the distance. The man silently wished them luck.

Muffled gunfire from within the hospital startled them.

"Here we go," said Nicholson, unslinging her rifle. Stevens tossed his cigarette and did the same. The man followed suit and unsnapped the flap of his holster.

More gunfire.

"I wonder how many are in there," said Stevens.

Another volley. Prolonged this time.

"Sounds like a lot," offered Nicholson.

The crash of an outside door opening violently. Close by, around the side of the building. They turned towards the sound. They could hear footsteps. Running.

"Oh shit," said Stevens softly. He and Nicholson lowered their rifles.

"Remember," she said calmly, "choose your targets."

The man drew his pistol and flicked off the safety. He took a deep breath and let it out slowly.

The sound of running grew louder and the mob rounded the corner of the building. The man was trying to count them when they spotted the trio and rushed towards them. Ten, he thought. Maybe twelve or fourteen. Filthy and wild looking, some still wearing the remains of hospital uniforms. One looked like it might have once been a doctor, he thought.

Nicholson was the first to fire. Stevens joined her, and the infected began to fall. Not fast enough. The man chose a target and drew a bead on its chest. He squeezed the trigger and the pistol barked. The infected he'd been aiming at dropped. He picked another. His aim wasn't as good this time and the infected kept coming, a blossom of blood at its shoulder where the man had winged it.

There were too many. "Get out of here, sir," said Nicholson as she squeezed off another burst. The man ignored her as he chose another target. This one dropped.

Then the infected were on them. The soldiers' rifles were useless in the close quarters. Stevens fumbled with his sidearm, unable to reach it as he grappled with the infected woman attacking him. The man rushed to him and fired his pistol point blank against the attacker's head. Blood and bits of bone sprayed both the men.

"Christina," said Stevens and they turned to look for Nicholson. She was down, and three infected crouched around her. They ran to her. The man pulled off one of her attackers. It fell back and snarled at him. He shot it in the face. Stevens put down another, and Nicholson fought her way back up against the strength of the remaining infected man. It was the doctor, the man saw. Stevens made to shoot it.

"Mine," said Nicholson, and dispatched it with her own pistol.

Six bite wounds. Even with fully prepared soldiers knowing exactly what to expect, there were still six bite wounds. It drove home the urgency of reproducing the vaccine before any refugees from the island arrived.

Nicholson was one of the injured. She was tough about it — perhaps tougher than her male colleagues might have been in the same circumstances. Both Stevens and the man hovered near her as she sat and let the medic dress her wounds.

"Sure about that vaccine, are you?" she asked the man jokingly. Masking her nervousness, he thought.

"Cole is still fine," he replied. "You will be too."

"Well if I'm not," she said, looking at Stevens, "make sure you do the right thing."

Stevens nodded. "I will, but you're going to be fine, Christina."

"All set," said the medic, having finished disinfecting and bandaging the bites. "They're pretty much superficial wounds. Have the dressings changed daily. We'll keep an eye on them, but you should be fine."

"See, you'll be fine," said Stevens.

Nicholson grunted and stood.

"Well, what now?" she asked the man.

"You sure you feel okay?"

"Yeah, I'm fine."

"Let's have a look inside then."

They walked to the entrance to the hospital. Already, troops were carrying out the bodies of infected. The garbage truck had been driven closer to the doorway, and the soldiers were tossing in the corpses as they brought them out. There seemed to be a lot of them, the man thought.

They met sergeant Gordon on their way in.

"You saw a little action," he said when he met them.

The man nodded. "We did."

"Uh hunh. Well, nice work."

"Thanks," replied the man. "I assume we're good to go have a look at the lab?" he asked.

"Yes, the building's clear. It was a little rough, but we got them all. There were a bunch holed up in the cafeteria. I'd recommend staying away from it. It isn't pretty."

I'll be it isn't, thought the man, if it was anything like the nest they'd encountered in the house.

"Thanks, we'll do that," he replied.

"Right," said the sergeant, "I'm going to go and see about getting the generator running. I'm imagining you'll be wanting power."

"We will. Thanks Sergeant," replied the man. He held out his hand. "Nice work today," he said. If he was supposed to be in charge, he thought, he probably ought to start acting like it.

Gordon looked surprised, but took the man's hand and shook it. "Thanks," he said.

The man nodded and led Stevens and Nicholson past the sergeant into the hospital. He realized he didn't actually know where the lab was, and had to stop to consult a map of the facility. Second floor, he saw. They'd have to take the stairs.

The hospital was, predictably, a mess. Much like the terminal building when they'd arrived on the mainland, there were papers and other litter strewn about. There was an awful lot of dried blood in evidence, but no corpses. The man wondered if the soldiers had already disposed of them or whether the infected had consumed them.

He led Stevens and Nicholson to a stairwell. They passed a makeshift barricade on the way to it. More dried blood both in front of it and behind it showed that it hadn't ended up doing much good in the end.

Into the stairwell and up to the second floor, the man borrowing Steven's Zippo to light the way. They found the lab easily by following the signs.

It was in better shape than the man had feared.

Someone — or several someones — had left in a hurry. There were overturned racks of test tubes, a small explosion of glass on the floor — from a flask, it looked like — and a half full coffee cup on one of the tables. No bodies or blood stains; the infected hadn't found any reason to enter the room. All in all, not too bad. It would be serviceable. All they needed was power.

As if in response to his last thought, the overhead lights flickered and came on. A centrifuge started spinning and the man walked over and turned it off.

He turned to Stevens and Nicholson. "Looks like we're in business here. Now let's hope that *Charlottetown* finds that helicopter."

The news continued to be good when they returned to the base. *Charlottetown*'s Sea King had located the evacuation helicopter; it had been damaged fleeing the atomic blast that obliterated St. John's and had set down on the island itself rather than risk crossing the strait.

Set down, in fact, in the same town that the man had recently left.

"Major Harry Marshall asked me to give you his regards if I met you," the Sea King's pilot told the man.

"Harry. He's okay?" asked the man, surprised.

The pilot nodded. "Holding down the town. Pretty bad over there. Fallout's blanketing the whole island except for the south west tip. They got the cloud from the strike on Goose, and you know about Gander and St. John's."

All gone, thought the man. All of their work and planning and all those people. Those that hadn't been killed instantly in the nuclear blasts would now suffer a slow lingering death. And there was nothing that his group could do for them. Even if they could get to the victims and move them here, there were no facilities to treat radiation sickness.

"Anyway," the pilot continued, "Major Marshall took care of the evac chopper's crew and passengers. Nothing he or his men could do about the chopper itself though. We brought the passengers and their equipment back with us. We're taking another run over for the crew in a little while."

"The lab people are here?" the man asked excitedly.

"In the terminal building with Major Dawson," replied the pilot.

"Thanks," said the man, "this is great news." He began to walk briskly over to the building, Stevens and Nicholson chasing after him.

"Any message for Major Marshall when we go back?" the pilot called after him.

"Yeah," shouted the man over his shoulder, "tell him to get his ass over here."

Three civilians were talking to Dawson when he entered the office. The man recognized Jeff Hall, Rebecca Chambers and Gene Newsham — people that he'd known back in the original labs from which he'd started his journey to where he was now. The conversation stopped and they turned to look at him when he burst into the room.

He could see that they didn't recognize him. He realized that to them, he must look very different than the last time they were all together. He'd almost certainly lost weight, his hair was shaggy and he had at least a couple of days' growth of beard. Not to mention the military issue clothing he wore and the fact that he (and his escort) still wore the blood from their battle back at the hospital.

After a moment, recognition suddenly dawned on Gene Newsham's face. "Oh my God," he said in wonder. He strode over and pumped the man's hand, grinning while he did it. Hall and Chambers followed quickly. The man was suddenly the center of attention with more handshaking, back slapping and a (ginger, gore avoiding) hug from Becky.

"We heard you might be here," said Gene, obviously the leader of the small group. "I can't tell you how good it is to see you."

"It's good to see you all, too," said the man, a grin of his own adorning his face. "We thought you might have gone down getting out of St. John's."

"It was close," agreed Gene, "but we had a great pilot, and the guy running that town where we landed…"

"Major Marshall," offered Dawson.

"Major Marshall," continued Gene. "He was a huge help."

The man nodded. "Harry's a great guy," he agreed. "So where are the rest of you?" he asked.

The smile fell off Gene's face.

"We drew straws for who got on the chopper," he said, "there wasn't room for all the equipment and all of the people. We knew you'd need the equipment. We also knew you wouldn't need all the people."

The man thought about the others he'd known from the lab, who he'd worked with and become friends with during the early days of the outbreak. They were radioactive vapor now, probably drifting over Europe. Half a dozen more to add to the monstrous death toll.

The man was silent. He couldn't think of anything to say to ease the pain, and probably guilt, these people were feeling.

"It's done now though," said Gene. "The best way we can make sure they didn't die in vain is to get the vaccine into production and help make sure the Plan succeeds."

The man laughed grimly. "The Plan is done, Gene," he said. "We're working on just surviving now."

Gene nodded. "Then the best way we can make sure they didn't die in vain is to make sure we survive."

The newcomers were eager to see the hospital's lab, but not so eager that they couldn't wait for the man and his escort to get cleaned up. A quick wash and a change into borrowed fatigues and he returned to them. Stevens arrived moments after him.

"Christina says she's exhausted," he said, "she's hoping we can do without her. She's gone to lie down."

The man guessed it was just the exertion of the day coupled with her injuries. He'd check on her later though.

"That's fine," he said, "she did have a rough day."

"All right, everyone," he said to the three scientists, "let's check out this new lab of yours."

He led them to his truck. He was momentarily amused to realize that he now considered it his. They squeezed into the back seat, with Steven's in his usual role of driver and him in the passenger seat. Doors closed, Stevens drove off out of the base.

They passed the signs of the troops' labors as they made their way to the hospital: red X's marked the doors of houses that contained bodies. Green X's marked the doors of houses that were clear. There were more red ones than the man would have liked. The troops must have had their hands full on their door-to-door searches. Unadorned doors still outnumbered the ones that the soldiers had visited. There was a lot of work remaining to secure the town, the man thought.

The scientists goggled out the truck's windows. They'd been evacuated early on, thought the man. They've never seen the aftermath. As if to underscore that last thought, they passed a garbage truck, visibly loaded with corpses. The newcomers stared after it.

The hospital, at least, had been secured. They were stopped at a checkpoint at the entrance to it. The man wondered what purpose a checkpoint served. Infected would be unlikely to stop at it.

The soldier at the checkpoint gave only a brief glance into the interior of the truck before waving them through. They pulled up in front of the hospital and Stevens switched off the truck and got out, retrieving his rifle and slinging it. The man and the scientists followed suit, and the man led them to the front doors which slid open as if by magic. He was glad to see the electricity was still on.

Most of the mess had been cleaned up — at least in the lobby — he was sure that there were still some scenes of horror elsewhere in the building. He led them to the elevator and pressed the call button. "The lab's on the second floor," he said. Gene nodded. They were all quiet. Still taking it in, thought the man.

The elevator arrived quickly and the doors opened. There was a red stain on the floor. Rebecca Chambers stared at it but didn't enter. "In we go," said the man. She shook her head as if to clear an unpleasant thought and entered the elevator with the rest of the group.

Minutes later they were in the hospital's lab.

"Kind of small," observed Jeff Hall skeptically.

"It's what we have," said the man.

The three scientists looked around.

"We'll have to clear out some of the stuff in here to make use of the equipment we brought, but we can make it work," said Gene. The other two scientists mumbled agreement.

"Good," said the man. "We'll move in the equipment tomorrow and you can get to work. Any ideas on timing? We're likely to start getting refugees from the island soon, and the faster they're inoculated the better."

"A few days?" said Gene, "A week? You know we're not going to be able to mass produce with this setup, right?"

The man nodded. "We do what we can."

Steven's radio chose that moment to squawk. He lifted it to his ear. Moments later, he handed it to the man. "Major Dawson for you," he said.

The man took the radio and held it to his own ear. "Yes, Major," he said.

"You'd better get back here ASAP," said Dawson, *"it's Nicholson. Looks like there might be something wrong with that vaccine of yours. We think she's turning."*

CHAPTER TEN

Infection

They rushed back to the base.

Nicholson had been moved to a utility room in the terminal building and was lying on a cot. Her wrists and ankles were tied to it and a pair of armed soldiers stood at the door.

"I'll examine her," said Rebecca, pushing her way to the front of the small group. Becky was an MD; one of several who'd worked in the labs, and now the only one remaining. As she knelt to examine Nicholson, the man could see evidence of the virus in the soldier: the sheen of sweat, the involuntary twitching of muscles and the wild, red, restless eyes. The eyes were always the giveaway. They finally rested on Stevens, who was looking at her in horror.

"Remember," whispered Nicholson, her gaze fixed on her partner, "you promised."

"I'll remember, Christina," he replied.

Rebecca looked up at the man from her examination and nodded.

"Outside," he said to her, and left the room, Rebecca following.

"How?" he asked when they were out of the room and out of earshot of the others.

She shrugged and shook her head. "I don't know. We'll need to do some tests...we should probably get her to the hospital so we'll have the equipment..."

"Can you help her?" he demanded, interrupting.

"You know the answer to that as well as I do," she replied.

"Damnit. Everything hinges on that vaccine working, Becky. Not to mention the young woman in there who trusted us and who's now going to have to be put down like a rabid dog."

"You know it didn't get a lot of testing," she said defensively. "And for all we know there could have been a screw-up with the shot she got."

"That's a good point," he said thoughtfully. "I'll get Dawson to start checking that. In the meantime, you're right — let's get her to the hospital."

The man stood with the small group of soldiers, barely hearing the ceremony as he stared at the coffin poised above the grave. The troops had made a good effort in putting together a proper funeral. Nicholson was only the third fatality so far, and the man thought they'd soon be getting more practice than they'd like. He'd try to remember, though, to suggest that they park the backhoe a little farther away next time. Its conspicuous yellow bulk took away some of the dignity of the ceremony.

He heard a quiet sniff beside him and turned his head slightly to look at Stevens. The young soldier was fighting back tears. The man reached out a hand and rested it on his shoulder.

"At least it was painless," he said quietly. Becky had made sure of that. The hospital's stocks of barbiturates were more than ample.

"She asked me to take care of it," replied Stevens with angst in his voice.

A sedative overdose was much surer, and kinder, than a bullet in the head, thought the man. That wouldn't make Stevens feel any better though.

"You were with her at the end, Charlie," he said, "and that's what matters."

The young soldier grunted. The man looked at him again, discreetly. He thought perhaps he looked a little less pained, and returned again to his own thoughts.

Rebecca, of course, had been unable to do anything for Nicholson, except try to make her comfortable and ensure that the end was painless.

The whole frantic trip back to the hospital, the restrained infected woman riding in the back of the man's truck with Stevens both guarding her and attempting to soothe her... a waste of time. They learned nothing in the hours remaining to them before they were forced to euthanize her.

News of Nicholson's infection — in spite of the vaccine — had raced through the troops. A lot of people were worried. The man was one of them. So far, the only good news was that none of the other bitten soldiers were exhibiting symptoms. They were being watched closely nonetheless, isolated and guarded.

The ceremony must have finished without the man hearing it — he saw the coffin begin to lower into the grave. He watched until it completely disappeared and turned to Stevens.

"Let's get back, Charlie." A pause before the young soldier nodded, and the two began to walk back to the truck. The man heard the backhoe start up behind them.

They made little progress towards finding the cause of the vaccine's failure in Nicholson. After several days and numerous blood tests, the other bitten soldiers were declared clean of the virus and allowed to return to duty.

They were certain she'd received the shot — Dawson had confirmed it in the medical records carried aboard *Charlottetown*, and there was no question about the competence of those who'd performed the injections.

There were many reasons why a vaccine might prove ineffective in an individual, and the man and the three scientists discussed all of them. There had never been, after all, clinical trials. This was it. Their biggest collective fear was the possibility that the virus had mutated, and a new strain was in the wild — one to which their vaccine provided no protection. The background radiation level had been climbing steadily as a result of the unbridled use of nuclear weapons, and the chance of mutation climbed along with it.

In the end, they did the only thing that they could, and began the setup to produce the vaccine in quantity, hoping that its failure in Nicholson was due to one of the many other possible reasons. An 85% effective rate was infinitely better than the alternative.

To play it safe though, Gene Newsham started down the path to finding out if their worst fears were true. But the equipment they'd brought with them was inadequate to the task, as was that of the hospital's small lab.

The man made the decision to send a team to search for the proper instruments in Halifax — the nearest city with a chance of success — and pressed *Charlottetown* into service to deliver them. It was the first time he'd exercised his authority and, to be honest, it had felt pretty satisfying. Gene had immediately volunteered for the expedition, as had Stevens, still smarting from Nicholson's death.

The man fervently hoped he'd see them again.

Regardless of the fears about the vaccine, there was still work that needed to be done, and the need would soon be pressing.

Harry would shortly be leading the townspeople under his protection across the strait.

Major Dawson had been in contact with Harry via radio, and the news hadn't been good. While the town had escaped the worst of the fallout, it hadn't escaped all of it. It was only a matter of time before radiation poisoning began to take its toll on the population. Add to that the cutting off of what meager supplies the town had been receiving and the need to evacuate became urgent. Even if they'd be leaving for the uncertain situation here on the mainland.

The educated guess was that they had a week — maybe slightly more, but not by much — until the evacuation would need to take place. Regardless of the gravity of the situation, the man found that the thought of seeing Harry again buoyed his spirits, and he found himself surprisingly cheerful as he discussed the logistics with Dawson.

"The door-to-door search is almost done," said Dawson, "I'm expecting it to be complete tomorrow."

The man hadn't been following the military's progress as well as he should have; the vaccine concerns had absorbed his attention.

"How bad was it?" he asked.

Dawson grimaced. "There were a lot more live ones than we'd expected, that's for sure. No more bites though, thank God."

The man nodded in agreement.

"And speaking of bites," continued Dawson, "what's the status of the vaccine. Are we in trouble or not?"

The man thought about it for a moment before replying. "Are we in trouble? Too early to tell. We're hoping that Nicholson's case was an isolated one, or at least a rarity. Seven cases where it worked versus one where it didn't are still pretty good odds. I wouldn't panic just yet."

"I'm not panicking," said Dawson, "I'm thinking about my men. Not to mention all those people Harry Marshall is planning to bring over."

"All those people. Do we know how many, exactly, is 'all those'?" asked the man.

"At least a couple of thousand," the last time I talked to him, "maybe as many as four."

"Thousand."

Dawson nodded. "That's right."

"Shit."

Dawson nodded again. "Exactly. We need housing, we need food, we need water, we need that vaccine. And we need it to work."

"In a week."

"Marshall figures that's all the time they have left. They're out of everything, and they're starting to get some cases of radiation sickness among the elderly and the very young. He's going to hold off as long as he can, but if the choice is certain death there or less certain death here…"

"I get the picture," said the man.

"So back to the vaccine."

"Jeff Hall and Rebecca Chambers are working to set up production. There's no way they're going to have thousands of doses ready in seven days. If I had to guess, I'd say ten to twelve weeks — if everything goes right."

"Damn," said Dawson quietly.

"Yeah. In the meantime, we're going to have to keep all those people away from even the slightest chance of infection. It'd spread like wildfire — just like in the beginning."

Dawson sighed. "So housing we can keep buttoned up. Quarantine, basically. It's going to take manpower;

not all of those refugees are going to appreciate being treated like prisoners."

"Major Marshall can help. The lab folks brought all the remaining vaccine with them. I'm certain there's enough to inoculate his troops."

"Good idea. I'll discuss it with him."

"Are you going to be talking with him soon?" asked the man.

"I was planning on giving him an update after our meeting, why?"

The man suddenly felt sheepish. "I wouldn't mind saying hello," he said.

Dawson chuckled. The man thought that it might have been the first time he'd seen the major do so.

"I keep forgetting you know each other. By all means. We'll call after we finish this."

"Thanks," said the man.

Dawson nodded. "So let's move on to how we're going to house and feed all these people."

"The whole pre-virus population of this town wasn't that much more than the number of refugees we'll be getting," the man observed.

"Somewhere around six thousand," agreed Dawson. "Most of whom are now corpses that we need to dispose of. That's the next priority. We can't move people into houses with dead infected in them."

"The virus won't be contagious in those bodies," said the man, "there's no reason that able-bodied adults can't help with disposal. With the proper precautions, of course."

"Okay, good," replied Dawson, "I didn't see any way my men would be able to clear out all of those houses in time."

"So a curfew with patrols until we have the vaccine in production?" asked the man.

"Yeah," replied Dawson, "we'll be spread thin, but I don't see any other choice."

"Which leaves us with power and water," said the man, "and food, of course."

"Power's out of the question for the time being. We can run generators as needed, but there's no way we're going to be able to bring up the grid. Looks like we'll have better luck with water though — we think we can get the well and pumps and the sewage treatment plant running."

"That's good news," said the man, "at least we won't have to worry about things like dysentery and typhoid and cholera. What about food?"

Dawson frowned. "We're going to have to forage across the bay in Sydney. The infected were bad enough here; it's going to be a whole lot worse in a city."

"We don't have a much of a choice though, do we?" said the man.

Dawson sighed. "No, we don't. It doesn't make it any more attractive though."

"I think that's it for what we needed to talk about. Getting all this done will, of course, be the number one priority for my men." He paused, and added: "As vaccine production will be for you and your people."

The man nodded.

"Okay, then," said Dawson, "let's get Marshall on the radio."

"Hello Harry," said the man. He heard a laugh of surprise, from the radio.

"*I was wondering what you'd got up to,*" replied Harry, "*it's good to hear your voice.*"

"And yours. I understand it's pretty bad over there."

"*We're holding on, and I guess it could be worse, but yeah, it isn't great here right now. I assume Major Dawson has filled you in on the situation.*"

"Yes," said the man, finding himself nodding even though he knew Harry couldn't see him, "we're doing everything we can to get ready for you. There've been a few bumps, but we think we have a workable plan."

The man glanced at Dawson, who was frowning. He supposed the major had wanted to deliver the news about the vaccine and the resulting restrictions that the refugees were going to have placed on them. Too bad, he thought.

"*I don't like the sound of bumps,*" said Harry, "*what kind of bumps?*"

"We had an infection in spite of the vaccine. We're looking into it; so far we think it's isolated. The real problem is that we won't have enough of it — the vaccine — for all of your people in time. The whole lot of you is going to have to be quarantined until we do. Aside from your men, that is. We have enough that the lab people brought over to inoculate your troops."

There was silence from the radio for a moment. Harry was thinking the news over.

"Well, we can't stay here," he said finally, *"we have more cases of radiation sickness every day, and we're almost out of supplies. Quarantine for thousands of people is going to be tough though."*

"Like you say, there isn't any choice. Major Dawson and I are hoping your men will be able to help out enforcing it."

"Of course," replied Harry. *"I'll have to break the news to the people here, and let them know what to expect and what's expected of them. Most of them haven't had any contact with infected except on TV. And I think a lot of them had pretty high hopes. How long for this quarantine?"*

"Ten to twelve weeks is our estimate to have the vaccine in production."

"Damn. This is going to be quite the operation."

"Yeah, I'm afraid it is, Harry." Major Dawson cleared his throat beside him and made a "wind it up" motion with his hand.

"Harry, I'm going to pass you over to Major Dawson now to go over logistics."

"Okay. It was good talking to you."

"Yeah, it was good to hear your voice as well," said the man. "Hey," he said, a final thought popping into his head, "how's Mary?"

"Mary's doing fine. I'll tell her you said hello — she's been wondering about you as well."

"Thanks Harry. Okay, here's Major Dawson. Take care."

"See you soon."

The next morning the camp bustled with activity as the troops worked to prepare for the arrival of the refugees, soldiers being marshaled and dispatched to their assigned tasks like clockwork. If nothing else, the man thought, Dawson was an extremely capable administrator. Preparation for the basics clearly well in hand, he decided to visit the hospital and check on the status of the vaccine production.

The town was now considered secure — as secure as they could make it, anyway — and Dawson no longer felt an escort was required. The man was fine with that; he'd never believed that he'd really needed one. He had, after all, managed just fine by himself crossing half of the country as it collapsed into chaos. Secure being a relative state though, he still wore his borrowed sidearm, and he'd made sure he had a full magazine before strapping it to his waist.

His truck was still where he'd left it last, and he got in and drove through the gate, nodding at the soldier guarding it as he passed through. It didn't take him long to arrive at the hospital. Another gate, another guard, and he was at the entrance. He parked in front of the doors, amused that he still felt a twinge of guilt at doing so in front of an EMERGENCY VEHICLES ONLY sign.

The doors opened as he approached them and he walked through, nodding to a bored looking soldier sitting at the reception desk, his rifle laid on it for easy access. Bored was better than the alternative, the man thought as he walked to the stairs and entered the stairwell, quickly climbing to the second floor and the lab.

Both Rebecca and Jeff Hall looked up when the man entered. He could see that they'd made good progress — a cell factory now occupied a prominent place in the lab, complete with the numerous valves, tubes and wires attached to it.

"We just finished setting it up and getting the seed virus into it," said Becky, following the man's gaze.

"That's great," replied the man, "you're making good headway."

"We'd be making a lot better headway if we had the proper facilities," said Hall with a sour note to his voice.

"It's what we have, Jeff," said the man, holding on to his temper. He knew that Hall had been sheltered from the effects of the virus from the very beginning. Maybe an excursion out with the troops would do his attitude some good. Something like the food foraging over in Sydney; that would get him some exposure to the world as it was now. He should probably hold off until they were farther along on the vaccine production though — just in case.

"Anyway," he continued, "a lot of people are counting on this, so we need to make it work."

Hall grumbled something to himself. Maybe that excursion needed to happen sooner, thought the man.

"Have we heard anything about Gene and his equipment search?" asked Rebecca, obviously trying to change the subject.

The man nodded. "*Charlottetown*'s in Halifax and Gene and the team are starting the search. It's going to be tough. We didn't use the gas there so they're going to be dealing with a full population of infected."

"How's that going to work?" she asked. "I remember what it was like when things were falling apart. Whole army units were overrun like they weren't even there."

"A small team, lots of stealth...it's been done before — like when we had to shut down that reactor in New Brunswick." He didn't add that a lot of those teams hadn't made it back. "We know that there *has* been some die off in the population as well. Not as much as we'd hoped for, but it should make a difference."

Rebecca looked at him, obviously unconvinced. He shrugged. "It's what needs to be done. There aren't really any other choices."

"That seems to be the theme around here," threw in Hall. The man felt his temper rise. Before he could react, Rebecca spoke again.

"Hey, I haven't eaten yet today. Feel like going and getting something? I'm sure Jeff won't mind watching the store."

"Sure," said Hall gruffly, "what else have I got to do."

"Come on," said Rebecca.

The man thought about it for a second. There wasn't anything else for him to do here, and Dawson had the preparations for the refugees well in hand. Plus, he was afraid he'd smack Hall if he stayed any longer.

"Okay," said the man, "come on."

'Something to eat' necessitated a drive back to the base. It wasn't as if there were any restaurants operating, the man thought, and sharing ration packs, for some reason, just seemed wrong.

Rebecca sat in the passenger seat of his truck as he drove them back, gazing idly out the window. She turned to him. "How are you holding up?" she asked.

He glanced over at her. There was a look of concern on her face. She wasn't making small talk. He answered truthfully.

"As well as anyone else is."

"You've managed to put yourself under more pressure than anyone else," she said. "As usual," she added with a faint smile.

"I'll survive."

"I'm sure you will. You have a knack for it. I think you need some relief from it though." Her smile seemed to have taken on a mischievous look. Or maybe it was something in her eyes.

What the hell? thought the man as they approached the base's gate, the guard waving them through. Becky was an attractive woman, but he'd never thought about her in any kind of romantic way; he'd been attached when they'd worked together previously. And since then…well, there'd been just too much going on.

He mentally shook his head. What was he thinking. She was probably making the observation as an MD.

"I'll be fine," he said finally, finding a spot and parking the truck. He noticed she was looking at him speculatively, but she said nothing in reply.

"Mess tent?" he said with a smile.

She laughed. "Sure."

They got out of the truck and walked to the mess tent. When they entered it, they saw that it was almost empty — only a few soldiers occupied the benches, those who for whatever reason had missed the regular mealtimes.

They walked to the serving line. A soldier dressed in cook's whites greeted them.

"Ma'am, sir," he said, "what can I get you?"

"What have you got?" asked the man.

"Well, you're in luck. The chili for lunch is ready. How does that sound?"

The man looked at Rebecca, who nodded. "It sounds fine," he said.

"Great," replied the soldier, "two orders of chili it is." He turned from them and started to prepare their meals.

"I hate chili," whispered Rebecca.

The man smiled. "You know what they say about beggars being choosers," he whispered back.

The cook returned with two trays, each containing a filled bowl and a bun. An unappetizing looking piece of cake — chocolate, maybe — accompanied them.

"There you go...drinks in the usual spot."

"Thanks," said the man, and he and Rebecca picked up their trays and turned and walked to the cooler where the drinks were stored, each extracting a bottle of water.

They found a table away from the few other occupants of the tent and sat down across from one another.

The man realized he was hungrier than he thought as he ate the chili. Rebecca, on the other hand, merely picked at hers.

"I can ask for something else," said the man, "I'm sure they can make you a sandwich or something."

"No, its fine," she replied, "none of us can really afford to be picky anymore, can we."

"Jeff Hall seems to be managing," he said.

Rebecca laughed. "He really pisses you off, doesn't he?"

The man grunted in acknowledgment. "He doesn't seem to realize how lucky he is."

"He does. The complaining is his way of blowing off steam. It just isn't very helpful to the people around him. He's really an okay guy. You didn't know him very well before, did you?"

"No," replied the man.

"Well, give him a chance. He's good at what he does."

"Fine," replied the man, "as long as I see results."

"You will. He's done most of the lab setup himself, you know. I've helped some, but he really knows what he's doing."

"Becky, I said it was fine. You don't have to keep selling the guy to me."

Rebecca didn't reply, and there was silence between them. The man finished his chili and saw that she was watching him. "Not going to finish your lunch?" he asked.

She pushed the tray away. "No. I guess I wasn't as hungry as I thought."

The man picked up the piece of cake. He knew that the cooks were trying to do the best they could with what they had available to them. He set it down again.

"Not going to eat your cake?" she asked with a look of amusement.

"I think I'll pass," he replied. "I guess you're not eating yours, either?"

She shook her head. "Anyway, we should probably get back to the hospital."

"Okay," replied the man, "I'll run you back."

They stood up and walked back to the front of the tent, emptying the lunch remains in a garbage can and placing their trays in the rack used for returning them.

Rebecca was quiet on the drive back. The man wasn't much for small talk, so the ride was silent and mildly uncomfortable.

"Are you going to come back up?" she asked when they arrived.

"I wasn't planning on it," he replied.

"Come on up for a minute," she said, "there's something I want to show you."

He followed her inside and up to the second floor. He was surprised when she walked past the lab and continued on down the hallway, choosing a different door.

He saw that it was an office of some sort. The large leather couch and other non-utilitarian furnishings suggested that it had belonged to someone high up. Maybe the hospital's administrator. A small open suitcase sat on the desk.

Rebecca nodded at the couch. "I use it sometimes rather than going back to the base. I can't bring myself to sleep in any of the patient rooms."

The man didn't blame her. The mess had been cleaned up and the bodies disposed of, but still... He walked over to the window and looked out. He heard a click behind him. He turned and saw that Rebecca had locked the door. As he watched, she began to unbutton her blouse.

"Becky, what are you doing?" he said, feeling the fool as soon as the words left his mouth.

"Like I said in the truck," she replied with that same mischievous smile he thought he'd seen earlier, "you're under an awful lot of pressure. I think it's time for you to get some relief."

CHAPTER ELEVEN

Refugees

The man drove back to the base, alone, the next morning. He felt unusually upbeat. Becky had been right, he mused.

As he neared the base, he passed a loaded troop carrier headed at speed in the direction from which he'd just come. The driver of the truck looked grim and didn't return the man's wave.

The man's mood changed instantly from one of optimism to one of trepidation, and he considered turning around and following the other vehicle. He had a sense of foreboding as to where it was headed. He was almost at the base, though. Best to find out what was going on first.

He pulled over to the side of the road ahead of the gate and exited the truck, walking over to the soldiers who stood around the mass of bodies. All infected, he saw, with wounds characteristic of the big guns of the armored personnel carriers parked nearby. Twenty, maybe twenty-five bodies by his quick count.

He identified an officer — a lieutenant — and approached him.

"What's happened, Lieutenant?" he asked.

The officer turned to look at the man. He looked worried.

"This group tried to breach the fence at dawn, sir. They almost made it through too. They surprised us."

"I thought the town was secured," said the man.

The lieutenant nodded. "It is, sir. This group came from somewhere else. That's why we were so surprised. We think they might have followed the foraging expedition back from Sydney."

This was bad, thought the man. The refugees were due imminently. He had another more immediate concern though.

"I passed a troop carrier on the road. Where was it headed?"

"To the hospital, sir. Major Dawson gave orders to up security there in light of this." The lieutenant gestured at the bodies.

"No indication that it — that the hospital — is in any danger?"

"No, sir. It's a precaution. That's all."

The man felt momentary relief. The vaccine production — and Becky — were safe for the time being.

He heard the sound of an engine. A truck arriving from inside the base. It stopped just back from the soldiers, and Major Dawson exited from the passenger side. Dawson spotted the man and strode up to him.

"Where the hell have you been?" he asked.

"I spent the night at the hospital," the man replied.

Dawson looked at him but said nothing. He could see the lieutenant attempting to hide a smile.

"Fine. Well, now that you're back, we need to decide how we're going to handle this new mess. Follow me back."

The man nodded. Dawson seemed flustered as he turned and marched back to his truck. Both the man and the lieutenant watched him go, the latter no longer trying to hide his smile.

The man turned and looked at the lieutenant. "Okay. And just what, exactly," he asked, "are you finding so funny?"

"I think you threw Major Dawson off, sir, and it isn't often that happens," replied the soldier.

"And how did I do that, Lieutenant?"

"Well, sir, you said you spent the night at the hospital..."

The man waited, saying nothing.

"Uhh, you can smell her shampoo, sir."

More frantic planning. The man was growing sick of it as they lurched from one disaster to another.

After the attack on the base's perimeter — seemingly a coordinated effort — they were faced with two choices: build up defenses around the town and hope that they wouldn't be overwhelmed in the near future, or wade in and conduct a war of extermination across the bay.

The troops would start leaving over the next few hours. It had been an easy decision for Dawson and the man to make. The thought of thousands of refugees — due to arrive in the next day or two — cut through by hordes of infected haunted them. They'd both seen that movie too many times already.

"How are we for ammunition?" asked the man. It was another of the lurking worries that he had now that they were effectively alone.

A frown from Dawson. "We'll be low after the cleanup in Sydney. We expected to be resupplied regularly. I have one of my officers working out logistics for an expedition to a base we can reach from here."

"They were all overrun," the man stated. Unnecessarily, he thought, as soon as he said it.

Dawson nodded. "It won't be easy. But then, what *has* been easy over the past months?"

The man grunted in agreement.

"Given this new situation, I think we need to ask Major Marshall to postpone the evacuation for a few days," said Dawson, moving to the next pressing subject.

The man shook his head. "They've cut it too close already. Dr. Chambers is already concerned about how we're going to treat all the existing cases of radiation sickness. We can't afford more."

Dawson thought about this for a moment before replying. "Certain death from radiation or possible death from infection."

The man nodded. "Exactly. We need to proceed with the evacuation as well as the operation in Sydney."

A sigh from Dawson. "Agreed. I'll update Marshall."

Each night, the man and others listened as the world died, the disrupted atmosphere still allowing their field radio to pick up broadcasts from around the globe. It made them grateful for their own situation. Daunting as it was, they were still far better off than anyone else out there.

They were, after all, more or less immune to the virus which had destroyed nations and was now tightening the noose around those who had managed, so far, to escape it. Small enclaves of humanity that through good luck or good planning — or both — found themselves sealed off from the chaos surrounding them and struggling to keep it that way.

But these enclaves were too far away and too preoccupied with their own situation to offer any assistance. And too far away to get the vaccine to.

Inevitably after each of these sessions, they returned quietly and individually to their lodgings, lost in their own thoughts.

The man stood with Rebecca, watching as the ferry approached the dock. With the majority of Dawson's troops currently across the bay, the two were needed to help the remaining soldiers with the refugees. Not to mention that the man wanted to be on hand to greet Harry, and Becky expected to be required to assist with the sick. Trucks stood by to transport those unfortunate souls to the hospital.

In the end, a large number of the town's inhabitants had decided to remain, taking their chances in the familiar settings of their homes rather than being uprooted and put into a situation which could quite possibly end up being worse than the one they were in. The man gave them even odds of surviving; the islanders were familiar with hardship and self-reliance and with the reduced population, they just might make it. He hoped they did, and he silently wished them luck.

The ferry docked and soldiers rushed forward to secure it to the moorings. They then stood back as the ramp lowered, spilling the air from the vessel's interior: the odor of a mass of humanity to whom hygiene had become a concern secondary to that of survival. A whiff of sickness underlaid the smell. From the frown on Becky's face, the man could see that she had caught it as well.

Once the ramp had lowered, a number of troops exited the ramp from the ferry and took up positions beside it. A barely perceptible nod from one of them towards the mainland soldiers. Guarding the exit rather than the entrance, the man thought. Conditions on board must be tense.

Finally, a familiar figure walked through the exit and paused, surveying the scene around him. His eyes landed on the man and he strode over too him, a broad smile on his face. He pumped the man's hand with enthusiasm, the smile still in place. The man found it infectious and realized he was also sporting what was likely a silly looking grin.

"Hello, Harry," said the man.

The worst of the sick were offloaded first.

Becky performed a cursory examination as each passed by. "Most of these people aren't going to make it," she confided to Harry and the man, "we'll try blood transfusions on the worst of them, but some are too far gone for us to do anything for them except to make them comfortable."

The man realized he hadn't made introductions.

"Rebecca, this is Major Harry Marshall."

Both Harry and Rebecca looked at him strangely.

"We already know each other," replied Becky. "Remember, we were stranded for a while, and Major Marshall took care of us until the helicopter from *Charlottetown* found us."

"Oh. Right. Of course," said the man. "So you know that Rebecca is an MD then, Harry?"

"I do," replied Harry, "and we certainly need one. A few of the hospital staff came over with us, but some decided to stay on the island. So we're a bit short staffed in the medical department."

"I'm happy to help," said Becky, "and I'll also be giving your men their inoculations as soon as things are settled here."

The last of the sick now on their way to the hospital, the remainder of the refugees had begun moving in an orderly fashion off the ferry, directed to large tents set up nearby.

"That might take a while," said the man, watching the progression. "What was the final count, Harry?"

"Roughly seventeen-hundred, not including my men."

The man nodded slowly. "That should make things go a little easier. We were lucky that so many decided to stay."

"We were at that," replied Harry, "but part of me feels guilty about leaving them over there."

"It was their choice," said the man.

They were interrupted by the sight of a raven-haired visage walking towards them, a youngster in tow, her eyes fixed on the man.

She reached the man and threw her arms around him, hugging him tightly. The man felt uncomfortable and returned the hug gingerly. He noticed Becky watching with one raised eyebrow. Finally, Mary broke the embrace.

"It's so good to see you," she said. "Harry told me that you were here, and that he'd talked to you, but I guess I didn't believe it until I saw it with my own two eyes."

"It's good to see you as well, Mary," replied the man. He bent down to ruffle Joshua's hair. "And you too, Joshua". The boy looked up at the man and smiled, a toy dinosaur clutched in his fist. Maybe the same one he had had when the three had first met in Alma, thought the man.

"Aren't you going to introduce me?" asked Becky, a faint look of amusement in her eyes.

"Uh, yes, of course," replied the man. "Rebecca, this is Mary. And the little one is Joshua. We met on the way to the island in the beginning, when everything fell apart. Mary was instrumental in getting that data to you folks in St. John's. Mary, Rebecca is a doctor who was working in the labs in St. John's and was evacuated here before it was destroyed."

"I'm pleased to meet you, Mary," said Becky, offering her hand to the younger woman, who took it almost with suspicion.

There was a feeling of tension between the two. The man knew that Harry felt it too, judging by the almost indiscernible look of amusement on his face. Harry decided to defuse the tension.

"Dr. Chambers, Mary has been invaluable in her assistance at the hospital back in Port-aux-Basques. I'm sure she'd be a big help here too."

"Well, that's wonderful," replied Becky, "we can certainly use all the help we can get. I need to follow those trucks," she said, gesturing at the departing makeshift ambulances. "Why don't you come along?"

Mary looked at Harry, who nodded. "Joshua can stay here with us until Mrs. Andrews debarks, and by the time you get back, we should have the two of them settled in and waiting for you."

Mary thought about it and then looked down at the boy. "Joshua," she said, "mommy has to go do some work at the hospital. Can you wait with these two men until Mrs. Andrews gets here?"

Joshua nodded. "Harry," he said. It was the man's turn to look at Harry with amusement.

"That's settled then," said Becky. "Come on, Mary."

The two women walked off to hitch a ride in one of the departing vehicles, leaving Harry and the man standing together.

"You dog," said Harry.

"I think I might say the same thing to you," replied the man.

Harry laughed. "You know they'll be talking about us."

The man nodded. "And it sounds like you and I might need to catch up on a few things as well." He bent down to the boy. "Why don't we go find Mrs. Andrews, Joshua."

"I should really be finding the commander on the scene," said Harry, as they looked for Mrs. Andrews.

"Dawson?" asked the man. "He's with the troops across the bay in Sydney. He sent word that he was on his way back to meet the ferry. I guess he was delayed."

"How is he?" asked Harry. "I mean, as a commander. How's he making out with this situation?"

"Well, he's quite a good administrator. A stern sort. Not the kind you'd imagine making friends with." The man laughed. "But he keeps things running smoothly and he keeps his men busy. They seem to have a lot of respect for him. So to answer your question, I think he's a good commander."

"Good to hear," replied Harry. "Look, there's Mrs. Andrews coming off the ferry."

Sure enough the man saw the elderly woman whom he remembered from his last night before the flight to St. John's. She was lugging a pair of suitcases that had seen better days, brushing off the attempts of soldiers to help her.

"I'm surprised she came," said the man.

"She's grown attached to the boy, and to Mary," replied Harry. "After having them in her home, I don't think she relished the idea of being alone again."

At this point, Joshua spied her as well and rushed over to her. She put down the suitcases and bent down to give him a hug. Harry and the man walked over.

She gazed at the man. A hard look. "You survived," she stated.

"I did at that," replied the man.

She grunted and then turned to Harry. "So now that I'm off that foul ferry, where are these homes that you told us about? And where did Mary go?"

"Mary went off to help get the sick settled in at the hospital. She asked us to ask if you could look after Joshua. Why don't we go and find out what accommodation is assigned to you and we'll take you there."

Mrs. Andrews nodded and picked up her suitcases, handing one to Harry and using her free hand to take the boy's. "All right then, men, lead on."

There were a few quiet mutters when Harry and the man jumped the queue to get Mrs. Andrews and Joshua their assignment and transportation to it. They were extremely quiet mutters though — the refugees had high regard for Harry after his and his soldiers' efforts in their town.

Harry's troops were, by necessity, restricted to the base itself until they were inoculated. It would make for close quarters, but it wouldn't be for too long; the remaining stores of vaccine were due to be delivered as soon as the sick were safely settled in the hospital. Becky was going to be run off her feet over the next few days, thought the man.

The man looked at his watch.

"Major Dawson should have been back by now," he said to Harry. "We should probably go and find out what the delay is — it isn't like him to be late."

"Lead on," replied Harry, and the two walked to the old terminal turned command post.

They entered the building, Harry returning the salutes given him, and went to what was now the communications room. The man nodded to the radio technician — Private Poole, he remembered.

"Any news from Major Dawson, Private?" he asked.

"Yes, sir," replied Poole, "he's on his way back. They had some problems with resistance."

"Resistance?" asked Harry. "What kind of resistance?"

"It sounds like they ran into an organized group, sir, someone blocked the road and they had some trouble getting out."

"Someone," said Harry.

"Infected, sir."

Harry looked at the man. "I thought their brains were basically burned out."

The man nodded. "But remember, we've seen pictures and we've heard reports of them cooperating with each other. We saw smaller examples of that here when we cleared this town. Nothing like this, though."

Poole watched the exchange. The man briefly thought that he might be saying too much, then discarded the notion. This shouldn't be a secret.

The man turned to Poole. "But they did make it out, Private, correct?"

"Yes, sir. Two injuries from what I've been told. They're being taken to the hospital. The rest of the convoy should be here real soon, sir."

"Injuries," asked the man, "what kind? Bites?"

"They didn't say, sir," replied Poole.

"We'll wait outside then. Thanks, Private."

"You're welcome, sir," replied Poole.

The man and Harry walked outside to wait. Neither man spoke.

"This is bad, isn't it?" asked Harry, finally breaking the silence.

"Yeah," replied the man absently. He was lost in thought, analyzing options.

"How bad?" asked Harry, hoping for elaboration. "After all, there are a couple of thousand people here now. People who haven't been inoculated and won't be for quite a while."

The man faced Harry. "It could be really bad, Harry, as in the end of us bad. They all but wiped us out, remember, and that was before they started exhibiting any kind of intelligence. If enough of them escaped the gas, if they're able to plan enough to lay a trap, even if it wasn't effective — this time — well, we're in a whole lot more trouble than we thought."

"So what do we do? Anything in that Plan of yours for something like this?"

The man shook his head.

"No," he replied, "we were counting on them starving to death and killing each other and then, when winter came, the rest of them would be wiped out. Maybe some stragglers come spring, but we would've had an easy time cleaning them up."

He paused, thinking for a moment.

"There was always the possibility that they'd regain some reasoning power. We knew that. The brain is pretty resilient. But we didn't think there'd be enough time for it to happen. That they'd die out first. So to answer your question: no, there wasn't anything in the Plan for this."

"Hmmmph," Harry grunted, "so we better start figuring out something ourselves."

The man nodded. "Without nukes or gas or, in not very long, ammunition."

"Maybe we're getting ahead of ourselves here," said Harry, "we should probably wait to hear what Major Dawson has to say before we assume the worst."

"Harry," replied the man, "at the point we're at now, with everything that's happened…well, sorry, but the only way any of us is going to survive is to *always* assume the worst."

The two men didn't have long to wait before they heard the sound of engines. The convoy streamed through the gates and came to a halt near the command post. Weary looking soldiers exited the mix of trucks and armored personnel carriers. The man noticed that more than a few of the soldiers wore NBC suits, the hoods folded back.

An equally weary looking Major Dawson walked towards them, having spotted the pair on the drive in.

"You must be Marshall," he said, extending his hand to Harry.

"I am indeed," replied Harry, "good to meet you at last."

Dawson looked at the man.

"We had some trouble that we need to talk about."

"I heard something about it," replied the man.

"Probably not everything," replied Dawson. "Let's go inside."

The three men re-entered the command post. Dawson led them to an office that he was now using, and closed the door, walking to his desk and directing Harry and the man to the chairs in front of it.

Before he could speak, there was a knock on the door.

"Come in," said Dawson.

A private cracked the door and stuck his head through.

"Sir, is there anything I can get you? Water or something?"

Dawson seemed to consider this.

"Yes, please, Private, water would be good. Enough for these two gentlemen as well if you please. I suspect we're going to be doing a lot of talking."

"Yes, sir," replied the private and pulled his head back outside, closing the door.

The man wanted answers.

"What happened, Major? I was told you ran into some kind of roadblock. And what was with the NBC suits?"

"I'll answer the last question first," he replied. "It seems that Sydney was hit with VX during the gassing runs instead of GB. It's still coating a lot of surfaces over there. Two of my men came into contact with it. We had the atropine injectors, so they're going to be okay. They're with your Dr. Chambers now."

My Dr. Chambers, mused the man, filing that thought away for later.

"We had suits with us — we've kept them in the vehicles since we landed. The men got into them as soon as we realized we had live residuals around us."

"Well, aside from the injured men, that's a good thing isn't it," said the man, "I mean, it should be keeping any surviving infected in check."

Dawson nodded.

"I would have thought so too. And so we come to the ambush."

"Ambush?" said the man, startled, "I heard a roadblock, but not an ambush."

"It was an ambush all right," replied Dawson.

A knock on the door again and at Dawson's command, the private entered carrying a pitcher of water and three glasses.

"Anything else, sir?" asked the private.

"No, that's fine, son, thank-you."

The private saluted and turned and left the room, closing the door quietly on his way out.

Dawson poured himself a glass of water and took a long drink.

"Yes, an ambush."

The man looked at Harry, seated beside him. Harry had said nothing so far. Aside from the problems in the refugee camp weeks ago, dealings with the infected were new to him and so he simply listened. The man could see the tension in his friend as he was hit with the reality of the situation here.

"It was a crude ambush," Dawson continued, "but it was unexpected. We'd dispersed throughout Sydney, working off a grid like we did here, and generally we found the same thing: lots of decomposing bodies — from the gas — some live ones in the buildings we checked. Buildings that it was obvious were being used. We took care of the live ones."

"We didn't secure Sydney by any means — that would take days, maybe weeks — but we were fairly certain that we wouldn't be seeing any overwhelming attack originating there. We'd reformed the column and were heading out when we came to some cars pushed into the middle of the road. They weren't there when we'd passed through earlier. When we stopped, the infected came at us. Twenty or thirty of them. The APCs made quick work of them and we cleared the roadblock and headed back."

The man felt some relief. Twenty or thirty. Not hundreds or thousands. And with the causeway blown weeks ago, and a wide channel between them and the rest of the province, no easy way for hoards from the bigger cities to get at them. The infected's newfound cunning was a worry, but it was a worry for another day.

Finished his story, Dawson took another sip of his water.

"So in your estimation, Major, we should be able to keep the refugees reasonably safe?" asked the man

Dawson nodded. "Curfew and patrols, as we discussed. But I didn't see anything over there to panic about."

"Well, that's a relief, Major. Thank-you," said the man.

It was Dawson's turn now.

"Major Marshall," he began, "I'm glad you finally made it. You and your troops will make a very welcome addition to the efforts here."

"And I can say with certainty that we're all happy to be here and eager to help," replied Harry.

Dawson looked at the man and continued. "And sooner, rather than later, we — or rather you — need to decide on the command structure."

The man felt surprise. He hadn't thought about this until Dawson said it. But he suddenly realized that there were two majors in the room and that the last instructions from St. John's had put him in charge. He tried not to let his surprise show when he answered Dawson.

"I understand that, Major, and we can have that discussion now, if you like, or we can have it later — say, this evening — after you've had a chance to recover a bit from your trip to Sydney."

Dawson grunted. "I'm not sure how much recovering I need to do myself, but I *would* like to see to the troops."

"This evening then. Say, seven o'clock. Back here," replied the man.

Dawson nodded. "Nineteen hundred it is."

The man turned to Harry. "In the meantime then, Major Marshall, why don't we go and see about getting your men inoculated."

The man and Harry drove to the hospital. By now, the man hoped, Becky would have the new patients mostly settled in and would be able to spare some time for them. If she couldn't, he'd have to give Harry's troops the injections himself. He was qualified for the task, but it wasn't something he liked to do. And people always seemed to complain that he jabbed them.

"Dawson's the right man to be in command, you realize," said Harry.

The man glanced sideways at Harry as he navigated the streets.

"And why do you say that?" he asked.

"He's done a damn fine job of keeping things running, from what I can see."

"He's definitely a good administrator," replied the man.

"A good commander too," said Harry, "and a good soldier."

"I take it you don't want the job?" asked the man.

Harry shook his head. "Honestly, this mess has taken a lot out of me. I'm more than ready to do something else."

"Something else like what?"

Harry thought for a moment. "Something in the field, I think. You know I've never had any direct contact with these infected, right? I've been safe over on the island for the duration. Well, safe from them at least." Sarcasm in the last sentence. The man knew it hadn't exactly been a picnic for Harry over there.

"Reconnaissance maybe? Or a supply run? We're running low on ammunition, you know."

"Something like that," replied Harry, "anyway, I'm fine with turning over what's left of my company to Dawson. And I'm fine being under his command as well."

Well that made things easier, thought the man.

"Okay, Harry," he replied, "we'll talk it through with him this evening."

They found Becky seeing to a patient. She finished up and joined the two men in the hallway outside.

"Most of these people are going to die," she said quietly to the man, "we don't have the facilities for bone marrow transplants — which is what they need. I'll do what I can with drugs and transfusions, but..."

Her voice dropped off and she shook her head.

"You'll do what you can, Becky, that's all any of us can expect." The man resisted the urge to hug her with Harry watching.

"You're here about the vaccine for Harry's troops, aren't you?" she asked.

The man nodded.

"Can you give the injections? I really don't want leave these people right now."

The man nodded again. "Sure, Becky, no problem." Given her predicament here, he supposed he could make it through fifty or so jabs.

"Let's get the vaccine then," she said.

They followed her to the hospital's pharmacy where she presented them with a box of bottles.

"This is it," she said, "the last of it until we start production. Don't drop it." She smiled, handing the box to the man.

"Syringes?" asked the man.

"Right, of course," she replied, finding more boxes, handing them to Harry this time.

"Are you coming back to the base tonight, Becky?" asked the man.

She shook her head. "No, I'll stay here."

"Okay," said the man, "don't wear yourself out though."

"I won't," she said, lying.

"Back we go then, Harry," said the man. As they turned to leave, Becky gave the man a quick peck on the cheek. Harry pretended not to notice.

"See you later, Becky," said Harry.

"Good-bye, Harry. Make sure he does a good job with those injections."

Harry laughed. "I'm sure he'll do better than I would."

The man finished the last of the injections, with a number of doses remaining. He slipped three of them into his pocket for use later. If Harry noticed his action, he said nothing. The idea of playing God made him uncomfortable, but he'd do it this once for purely selfish reasons, to avoid the pain of losing others who were close to him.

If there had been any complaints about his technique, he hadn't heard them from the soldiers he'd injected and who were now as immune as the rest of them. As he'd said before, an 85% effective rate was infinitely better than the alternative.

"Almost done," he said to Harry, who'd stood watching as his troops were immunized, speaking amiably with each soldier as their turn came.

Harry sighed and then nodded, rolling up his sleeve. The man injected him and Harry winced. "You need some lessons from Dr. Chambers," he said.

The man smiled. "Hopefully she'll do these the next time."

They noticed a soldier walking briskly towards them. Not one of Harry's. They faced him, waiting until he arrived. They could see his urgency, but the look on his face gave no indication of new disasters. He looked excited.

"Sirs," he said, arriving in front of the man and saluting both him and Harry. Harry returned the salute. The man simply nodded.

"Sir," he said directly to the man, his face animated, "there's someone at the gate. They said they want to talk to whoever's in charge."

CHAPTER TWELVE

Others

The newcomer's name was Morgan James. Harry, Dawson and the man sat watching as he methodically devoured a quick meal prepared for him by a very surprised cook and delivered to Dawson's office by an even more surprised private.

"You people've caused a lot of trouble you know," stated James between mouthfuls.

The three other men looked at each other, silently deciding who would speak. So far they'd managed to get little information out of the scruffy — but clean — visitor who sat with them; late fifties or early sixties, guessed the man, healthy looking if a bit lean. James had demanded food before talking to the three, saying he was tired and hungry after his trip there, and that the least they could do was feed him since he'd walked all that way on his own.

The man saw that Harry and Dawson were now both looking at him. He sighed inwardly. I guess I'm in charge after all, he thought. He cleared his throat.

"What kind of trouble are you referring to, Mr. James?" asked the man.

James stopped his fork midway to his mouth and lay it on his plate instead, looking directly at the man for a few moments.

"Well, that damn gas of yours was bad enough, but now you've gone and stirred up those things and it's making it damn hard for everyone else." He stared at the man for a moment longer and then picked up his fork again and resumed eating.

The gas, thought the man. They'd dropped leaflets beforehand in places where they'd thought there might be survivors, but maybe they'd missed whatever community James was from. And they had used VX in the outlying areas, and VX stuck around for a long time.

"Are you still having problems with the gas?" asked the man.

James shook his head. "Not for a while," he said through a mouthful of food, "but we lost a bunch of people to it and folks are still pissed off at you all."

He could imagine they would be, thought the man, but it sounded like that particular problem was over with and he was eager to get to James' second statement.

"What do you mean 'stirred up those things'," he asked, "how have you managed to avoid them so far? And what's happening now?"

James finished what was left on his plate and pushed it away. "Any chance of some coffee?" he asked.

The man nodded to Harry who left the room briefly, presumably to ask one of the soldiers stationed outside the door to fetch coffee for their visitor.

"On its way," replied the man once Harry had returned. "Now, Mr. James, are you going to answer our questions?"

James sighed. "I suppose it's time," he said.

"There isn't a whole lot to tell, really. When things went all to hell a bunch of us headed up into the mountains. We do some hunting up there and we know the area and there's shelter. Those of us with families brought them along. We're pretty much off the beaten path and we weren't bothered by those things or by ordinary folks looking for a place to hide. Well, we've had a few, but nowhere near as many as the towns and cities got, and we managed to keep things going by hunting and by foraging in some of the closest small towns."

They were interrupted by a private, who entered the room after knocking, to deliver James' coffee. James took it from the young soldier and nodded his thanks.

"Those things you talk about — we refer to them as infected," stated the man.

James took a sip of his coffee and shrugged. "Whatever you want to call them. They're bad news. We lost a couple of good men to them early on when we were foraging. We know how bad they are: we followed the radio before everyone stopped broadcasting."

"Anyway," continued James, "we lost more people after you idiots dropped that gas. It hung around a long time. I don't know why you couldn't have warned us." He stared at the man for a moment as if the gas was personally his fault. The man supposed that in a way it was. It had been in the Plan.

"I'm very sorry about that, Mr. James," replied the man, "every effort was made to inform any survivors we knew about that we were going to do what we did. We dropped tons of paper leaflets beforehand. I guess you were so well hidden that we didn't know about you."

James seemed to take some satisfaction in that. Pride, maybe. "Damn right, we were," he said defiantly.

"So now, Mr. James, what situation are you in with the infected now? What's happening?"

James resumed his former bitter demeanor.

"Yeah. So after you people started messing around here, you stirred them up. All of a sudden we've had dozens in our area where there weren't any before. Every day we kill a bunch of them, try to keep them away from the camp. It's exhausting, and sooner or later a big group of them is going to come through and that'll be it for us."

"How did you know we were here?" asked the man.

"How could we not? The noise carries a long way you know — your big guns and sirens and engines. We sent a couple of guys down to have a look a few days ago, see what you were doing, and they came back and told us about all the killing and burning you were doing."

"Why didn't they make themselves known?" asked the man, "Maybe we could have helped."

James shrugged. "I'm making us known now, aren't I."

The man looked at Harry and Dawson, who were both following James' tale with fascination. He looked back at the visitor.

"So, Mr. James, having walked so far, and announced yourself and told your story...what exactly do you and your people want?"

James laughed. "You folks aren't so bright, are you? Isn't it obvious? We want you to come and clean up the mess you made."

The three men sat in Dawson's office. They'd excused themselves from their visitor, leaving a pair of soldiers in their place. James seemed harmless enough, but it wasn't worth taking any chances.

"What do you think?" asked Dawson of the man, "Does his story make sense? Could we have driven infected to his camp?"

The man nodded. "It's possible. Remember, we haven't come across as many as we'd expected. Maybe they were smart enough to get out in time. Head elsewhere."

"And that camp of theirs. Plausible? That they could hide out for so long?"

The man nodded again. "We know that the infected mostly stuck to roads during the initial outbreak. We thought it had something to do with old habits still wired in their brains. Plus it was the path of least resistance. It makes sense that they wouldn't have spent much time wandering around in the mountains."

"And now they are."

"And now they are. Maybe they caught a scent, followed some scout or foraging party." The man shook his head. "Who knows how they found them — the point is that they did."

"Marshall, what do you think?" asked Dawson.

Harry cleared his throat.

"Well, Mr. James' story rings true to me. We should help them out since it *was* probably our fault they're in the situation they're in. The problem is that even if we could spare the troops, we're low on munitions. We have our own people here that we have to protect." Harry looked at the man. "Sorry," he added.

The man thought for a minute while Harry and Dawson watched him.

"We send troops. As many as we can spare," he stated. "It's the least we can do, and some recon in that area would seem like a good idea. Not to mention that these are locals who could probably help us figure out a way to survive through the winter."

"I wish we had *Charlottetown*'s helicopter," he said. He looked at Dawson. "What's the latest word from them?"

"In the last contact with them, which was yesterday, they reported that they were waiting on Dr. Newsham to return to the ship. He'd managed to find most of what he'd needed and it was just a matter of transporting it back."

"Good news," said the man.

"I'll get an update after we're finished here," offered Dawson.

The man nodded once to Dawson and then turned to Harry.

"You'll lead the expedition."

Harry didn't look surprised. A faint smile adorned his lips.

"Yes, *sir*," he said.

"See what you can do with them. Train them, get fortifications up, whatever you can think of."

"I can do that."

The man sighed. "Okay, gentlemen, we have a little bit of a plan. Now let's talk to Mr. James."

The soldiers whom they'd left with James were seated, talking with him, when the trio re-entered the room. Both sides were hungry for information, thought the man. The two privates stood up when they entered, looking slightly chagrined.

"That'll be all, boys," said Dawson, and the two soldiers saluted and left the room, closing the door behind them.

"Sounds like you've got a bit of a mess of your own," said James, as Harry, Dawson and the man once again sat down.

"We have some challenges ahead of us," replied the man.

James laughed. "Challenges? How are you planning on feeding all those people you've brought over? Winter's not far away, you know."

"We're working on it," injected Dawson flatly.

James grunted. "Well, good luck with that."

The man decided to steer the conversation away from their own problems for the time being.

"Mr. James," we've decided we're going to try to help you out. "Major Marshall will lead a mission to your camp and help you with defenses and training and clear out as many infected as they're able."

"How many soldiers?" asked James.

"Two sections," replied Dawson, having already calculated how many men he could spare.

"About sixteen men," Harry translated for James' benefit.

"Sixteen men?" stated James with some incredulity. "That's it? We're going to need a lot more than that."

"That's all we can offer you, Mr. James," said the man, "frankly, we're low on ammunition as well as other supplies, and sending more troops would put us in very dangerous territory. As you yourself pointed out, we have a lot of people to protect."

James leaned back in his chair and looked thoughtful. "Well, I may be able to help you out on one of those problems."

The man raised his eyebrows. "And how would that be, Mr. James?"

"Well, it turns out that I know the whereabouts of a convoy that got overrun towards the end. An army convoy. It's still sitting there. We've been getting ammunition from it and some other stuff, but there's lots still there. And lots of big stuff we can't use. I could show you where it is."

The man saw Dawson and Harry looking at each other. Depending on what was left in the convoy, it would certainly be a lot easier to get to than some army base hundreds of miles away.

The man smiled at James. "I think, Mr. James, that we have the beginnings of a mutually beneficial arrangement."

"You're sure you want to come along?" asked Harry. "I mean, aren't you needed here?"

"For what?" replied the man. "Dawson has things under control with the refugees and defenses, Becky's keeping things ticking along at the hospital...I'm kind of a fifth wheel, Harry."

Harry thought about it for a moment, probably considering making some comforting noise.

"Yeah, you're right," he said instead.

The two armored personnel carriers ('Light Armored Vehicles', or 'LAVs' as the man had been corrected) sat waiting for them.

"Where's Mr. James?" asked the man.

"Inside already," replied Harry.

The man had seen the vehicles around constantly, but this was the first time he'd taken a close look. Perhaps because he'd be inside one himself for what might end up being a long time.

The LAV was a big green box about six feet high, plus a turret with a large gun and four big off road wheels on a side. There was a soldier in a hatch in the turret, and he waved Harry and the man to the back where a small door swung open.

"Last chance," said Harry.

"Let's go," replied the man.

The man awkwardly climbed through the hatch. Hands reached out and hauled him in. Inside were soldiers in full combat gear facing inwards on seats against the sides, along with Morgan James, who looked annoyed and uncomfortable. As they squeezed to make room for him and Harry, he looked around. The interior walls were painted white, interrupted by what he assumed were radios, and other green boxes whose function he could only guess at. Forward was a round platform on which he could see the legs of the two men standing in the turret.

The man struggled forward past the knees of the soldiers, making for the space cleared for him. Moments after he sat down, Harry squeezed in across from him. He was handed a headset and given quick instructions on how to use it.

"Tighter than I expected," said the man. He saw some of the soldiers smiling after he said it. He decided not to make a comment about the smell.

Harry nodded. "Not the most luxurious ride, but definitely the safest. Anyway, we should only be in here an hour or so."

One of the men in the turret turned and dropped down, quickly scanning the men until he saw Harry.

"Sir?" said the soldier.

"We're ready, Corporal. Move it out."

The trip was long enough that the man felt himself dozing off; the gentle rocking of the vehicle coupled with the steady sound of the engine, muffled by the headset, and the press of warm bodies lulling him almost to sleep. He looked around the LAV's interior and saw that some of the soldiers had indeed taken the opportunity.

The LAV slowed and he felt it make a turn, then accelerate slowly, the new road clearly of lower quality than the one they'd traveled on for the past hour. The pitching and bucking of the vehicle woke the soldiers who'd been sleeping and who instantly became alert.

Another fifteen or twenty minutes later, the man felt the vehicle slow again — thankfully, he thought; this last part of this trip had put him in mind of his flight from the carrier, what seemed like ages ago, and he was certain that he'd be sporting more than a few bruises from his impact with the hard, sharp objects bolted to most of the walls around him.

The LAV came to an abrupt stop and the man was thrown violently against the soldier beside him. He heard the sound of small arms fire from outside: the crack of two bullets snapped outside the hatches and another ricocheted off the armor with a vicious whine.

"Shit!" he heard, then the hum and a thump as the turret traversed, immediately followed by Harry's voice in the intercom: "Don't shoot!" just as three machine gun rounds chattered down range.

"Cease fire!" from at least two voices from the headset, as more bullets impacted the armor from outside. Then silence.

The man looked at Harry, who looked back at him, shaking his head. "Not quite the reception I was expecting, he said."

"What now," asked the man, "do we have a white flag?"

"We don't usually carry those," replied Harry with a grimace. A sigh. "Mr. James and I will go out and clear this up."

"Sir," interjected the corporal commanding the vehicle, "shouldn't we dismount and secure the area first? You're taking a big risk going on there on your own."

"It's a misunderstanding, Corporal, and these folks are understandably jumpy. Let's not make the situation any worse than it is."

"Yes, sir," replied the soldier, although he clearly didn't agree with Harry.

The man heard a flurry of commands over the headset, and saw the soldiers around him tensing in preparation for action but remaining in their seats. The big ramp opened with a loud bang.

"Mr. James," said Harry, "why don't we go and meet your people."

With some effort, Harry extracted himself from the soldiers surrounding him and rose; Morgan James doing the same but with a look of apprehension on his face. The two men made their way to the ramp and slowly walked down it, Harry first, his arms raised to show he was unarmed. The man heard more orders in the headset: if things went badly out there, James' people would not be treated gently by the soldiers.

The tension was thick in the LAV as the situation was described in play-by-play detail by the commanding corporal over the headset. Finally: "The Major's signaling it's clear. Dismount!".

The troops somehow scrambled out of the LAV, one or two stumbling and then recovering. The man followed behind them and saw them forming arcs around the vehicles. He looked around him, taking in the encampment: six or eight trailers and RVs parked around a wooden cabin like moons orbiting a planet. A hunt camp, he thought. He saw Harry standing with Morgan James along with several other men. While he watched, Harry turned and made a motion to the troops, who relaxed and lowered their rifles, then waved to the man to join him.

The man walked over to the knot of scruffy looking men and shook each of their hands as Harry introduced him. They eyed the man suspiciously.

"You're behind this, then," said one of them. Before he could speak, Harry answered for him.

"No, he's the one who's been trying to get us out of it," he replied.

"Funny way of doing that," said another of the men, "we'd be doing just fine here if it wasn't for you stirring things up. Not to mention that gas."

It was James' turn to speak up. "I've been through all that with them, George, leave it be. They're here to help us."

An unconvinced grunt was the only response.

"Mr. James," said Harry, wanting to defuse any arguments before they could start, "now that we're here, why don't we get the troops settled in and get started."

'Security through obscurity' was how Harry described the camp. No natural barriers and no way to easily fortify it: its remote location the only protection against the infected.

The camp's occupants numbered twenty-eight according to James. Families and extended families — friends of James, who owned the cabin around which the trailers and RVs orbited. The group's armament consisted mostly of hunting rifles and shotguns, along with a number of military rifles salvaged from the convoy they'd discovered, and they'd organized a system of patrols which seemed to have impressed Harry.

Now, sitting around a table in the cabin along with the camp's leaders, the man watched as Harry delivered the hard truth.

"Mr. James," began Harry, "you've probably already started to find out how hard this location is to defend. Aside from setting up claymore mines, I don't see that there's much that we can do to make it better. Your patrols are doing the job for small groups of infected, but it wouldn't take much for them to be overwhelmed."

James opened his mouth to answer and was interrupted by the sound of gunfire and yelling from outside the cabin, sporadic cracks of rifle fire followed by the rattle of automatic weapons, and finally the big guns from the LAVs. The men scrambled from the table, pausing only to grab their own weapons, and rushed out the door, Harry and the man close behind.

A large group of infected, twenty-five or thirty, guessed the man, were rushing through the woods towards the camp, soldiers and the camp's inhabitants together in a line methodically — and to the man's eye, calmly — cutting them down. It was over quickly, and the defenders moved forward to make sure that there were no survivors.

Harry and the man walked to James who was surveying the scene with concern.

"We haven't seen this many before," he said, eyes wandering over the bodies of the infected who'd made it almost into the camp itself. It was obvious to all that without the additional firepower of the soldiers, the defenders would have been overrun.

"Mr. James," said Harry, "as I was saying earlier, it wouldn't take much for you to be overwhelmed. You have a very capable group here. Why don't we talk about your people joining up with ours?"

The attack had been a rude wake-up call to the camp's inhabitants. Now once again sitting around the cabin's table, the discussion was no longer about how to fortify the camp, but how and how soon to move its people to Sydney.

"We'll put it to a vote," said James, "but I'm guessing that after today there won't be any objections to joining up with you folks. We should move out tomorrow, early as possible before another mob of your infected decide to come through."

Harry nodded. "It's a good plan, Mr. James. And your people will be a big help to us." The man nodded in agreement.

A knock on the cabin door. James stood and opened it, motioning a soldier inside.

"Radio for you, sir," said the soldier, looking at the man.

The man glanced at Harry, who raised his eyebrows. "Not for the Major?" he replied.

"No, sir. It's Major Dawson. He asked for you."

The man nodded and stood up, following the soldier outside to the lead LAV. This won't be good, he thought, as he entered the vehicle.

A second soldier handed him a headset. The man put it on with apprehension.

"Major Dawson," he said, without preamble.

"*I've just talked to* Charlottetown," said Dawson, "*bad news, I'm afraid.*"

The man waited, knowing what was coming.

"*I'm sorry to tell you that Dr. Newsham and the team with him were lost,*" continued Dawson.

The man sighed. "Lost how, Major?"

"*They were overwhelmed at the pickup point. The Sea King saw it all. No chance of survivors.*"

"And the equipment? The instruments they were bringing out?"

"*The Sea King crew wasn't sure. They couldn't land then and it's still too hot. They thought there might be something left behind, but with the violence of the attack they weren't sure how damaged the equipment was.* Charlottetown *is asking for orders.*"

The man closed his eyes. More deaths. He remembered Private Stevens at Christina Nicholson's funeral. He remembered Gene's enthusiasm. He thought about the setback this would cause in understanding the limitations of the vaccine — or the mutation of the virus.

"*Still there?*" Dawson's voice at the other end of the connection shook him out of his thoughts.

"Yeah," replied the man. "Tell *Charlottetown* to come home."

"*You don't want to try for the equipment?*"

"No. I don't want to lose anyone else on this. And it's likely all ruined anyway. It's pretty delicate stuff."

"*I'll pass the orders on.*"

"Thank you, Major."

"*Some good news, by the way. Atmospherics are improving — we've managed sustained contact with North Bay.*"

The man braced himself to hear of whatever dire situation that now faraway base was in.

"What's their situation then, Major?"

"*Better than we expected. That near miss they took landed about seventy-five miles east of them. The prevailing winds carried away most of the fallout.*"

Dawson paused before continuing. The man could hear the excitement in the major's voice; a first in his dealings with him.

"*The base has been receiving aircraft and units that made it through the war. They say they have the base secured and are finishing doing the same with the town. The extra troops and aircraft arrived just in the nick of time.*"

The man was shocked and couldn't think of an immediate response. He'd thought, as they all had, that North Bay was out of the picture, the people there doomed to starvation or worse. Now though, this changed everything. Still, North Bay might as well be on the moon with the distances involved through what was now effectively enemy territory. He voiced this to Dawson.

"I didn't tell you the best news yet. They took in four Hercules. Which means airlift capabilities."

And just like that, thought the man, it looked like there just might be a way out of this.

The next morning was a flurry of activity as the camp's inhabitants prepared to leave their sanctuary of the past months. A sanctuary which was now anything but.

The man discussed the revelations about North Bay privately with Harry. Both were excited, but decided to avoid getting the others' hopes up. There was a lot more information they needed and, if it really was as good as it sounded, a lot more logistical planning to do.

If North Bay didn't pan out, they'd still need the ordinance from the abandoned convoy, and one of the LAVs had left early for it with the hope that its crew could be back at the base before nightfall with the supplies. While it hadn't been discussed specifically, no one was comfortable with the idea of traveling at night.

The decision to abandon the camp having been made, its people wasted no time and it wasn't long before the man found himself once again on the road;

this time, however, riding in a pickup truck with Morgan James, directly behind the remaining LAV. There had been concerns over his safety from Harry, but the man had dismissed them, explaining that he wanted to speak with James, but really wanting to avoid another jostling in the armored vehicle.

The line of vehicles rolled out, the menacing looking LAV leading, followed by lumbering RVs and trailers. The man looked out the window as the forest closed in around the gravel road and for a brief second, too quickly for him to react, he glimpsed a figure: by its dress, demeanor and appearance clearly one of the infected, watching the vehicles go by, the unmistakable glint of intelligence in its eyes.

CHAPTER THIRTEEN

Quiet Preparations

Mary hung her light jacket on one of the hooks just inside the door of the small house she'd been assigned with Joshua and Mrs. Andrews. The slight chill in the evening air gave warning that summer was ending, with all of the associated problems that would face the community as a result. She heard her ride from the hospital back out of the driveway, then the sound of the car's engine fading into the distance as the driver — a young soldier — headed to the base.

She was exhausted from her work in the hospital and the hopelessness of some of the cases she tended to. She wondered how Becky kept her positive demeanor. Years of practice, she supposed.

A voice, Mrs. Andrews', called 'Hello?' from the kitchen. Mary walked the short distance to it and saw the older woman cleaning. She did a lot of cleaning; the faded red stains in some of the rooms told the story of the home's previous occupants and foreshadowed the possible fate of its current ones.

"Hi, Mrs. Andrews. I guess Joshua's asleep?"

"He went down about half an hour ago," replied Mrs. Andrews, "he wanted to stay up to see you, but he just couldn't do it."

Mary smiled sadly. "This work at the hospital isn't going to last forever, but I still feel bad being away from him so much."

"Don't be too hard on yourself, dear. He doesn't understand exactly what you're doing, but he knows you're helping people. He'll be fine."

"I hope so," replied Mary.

"Did you eat?" asked Mrs. Andrews.

"Yes, I had something quick at the hospital."

Mrs. Andrews frowned. "I can only imagine. Why don't I fix you something proper."

Mary shook her head. "No thanks, Mrs. Andrews. I'm really not that hungry right now."

The truth was that she was rarely hungry these days. The refugee situation put her painfully in mind of the ill-fated camp back on the island; the smells and sights and the air of fear and frustration dragging her back to that time.

"You need to eat," said Mrs. Andrews, "you're wasting away, girl."

A knock on the front door saved her. "I'll get it," she told Mrs. Andrews and walked out of the kitchen back to the house's small foyer. It was Rebecca Chambers, she saw through the door's paned window. She looked distracted, as if she was in thought.

"Hi Mary," said Rebecca when Mary opened the door, "sorry to bother you so late."

"It's fine," replied Mary, "come in." She motioned Rebecca into the living room. Mrs. Andrews entered from the kitchen, curious about the evening's caller.

"Hello Dr. Chambers," she said.

"Hi Mrs. Andrews," replied Rebecca, "sorry for dropping by so late. I have some news for Mary."

"Not to worry, dear," replied Mrs. Andrews, "should I put on some tea?"

"Yes, please, if you don't mind," said Mary, following behind Rebecca. "Have a seat, Doctor."

Rebecca chose a comfortable looking armchair and sat. Mary sat near her on the room's couch.

"So what brings you by, Doctor?" asked Mary.

Rebecca laughed. "You need to start being less formal, Mary," she said, "Rebecca, or Becky is just fine."

Mary smiled. "Rebecca. Sorry, it's hard to get out of the habit."

"I know," replied Rebecca, "anyway, I have some news that I thought you might like to hear. It's good news, by the way."

"You don't look like you have good news," replied Mary.

Rebecca looked startled and then chagrined, having been caught in whatever thoughts were going through her head.

"Sorry," she said, "I also received some bad news. A colleague — you never met him — was lost on a mission."

"I'm sorry," said Mary.

"He knew the risk he was taking. But still..." She paused, then visibly dismissed the thoughts with a shake of her head. "Anyway," she continued, "that's not why I'm here. I have some very good news."

"I could use some good news," replied Mary.

"I thought you might." Rebecca took a deep breath. "So the men will be on their way back tomorrow. No injuries, and they're bringing back some survivors."

Mary felt relief and realized that she had indeed been worried about the two men who had helped her and Joshua — taken care of them, really. She became conscious of the fact that she was rubbing the still-sore injection spot on her arm from the vaccine that the man had given her and Joshua and Mrs. Andrews.

"That *is* good news," said Mary, moving her hand to her lap.

Rebecca nodded. "And it sounds like the survivors will be able to help around here. They've toughed it out on their own long enough that they've developed skills that we could really use."

Mary nodded. She was less sure about the last bit, but she supposed that anyone who'd survived this disaster on their own would be a good addition.

"There's more," said Rebecca, "and I'm not really supposed to talk about it, but given, you know, your relationship..."

Mary felt her face grow warm. Damn, she thought, I'm probably blushing.

"Anyway," continued Rebecca quickly, seeing the younger woman's discomfort, "it sounds like there's a chance we might be getting out of here."

"Getting out? Where? How?" asked Mary.

"To the military base in North Bay," replied Rebecca.

"Ontario?"

"Yes. There's a big old Cold War bunker there. It's huge. It was shut down, but when things started looking really bad there was a big push to get it running again. They made it just in time, according to Major Dawson. They were missed in the war, and it turns out they had a big influx of planes and troops that survived. As a result, they've managed to hold on and actually secure a large area. Large enough to support all of us is what they told Dawson."

"Keep it to yourself for now," she finished, "the Major wants to make sure everything checks out and we can actually move everyone before it becomes public knowledge."

"Before what becomes public knowledge?" Mrs. Andrews asked as she entered the living room with the tea.

"Oh, just some hospital stuff, Mrs. Andrews," said Rebecca.

"Hmmmph," was Mrs. Andrews' skeptical reply as she eyed the two women. She set the two mugs of tea on the coffee table before Mary and Rebecca.

"Thank you, Mrs. Andrews," said Mary.

"You're welcome, dear," replied the older woman. "I think I'm going to head off to bed. It's been a long day."

"Good night, Mrs. Andrews," said Rebecca.

"Yes, good night, Mrs. Andrews," said Mary, "see you in the morning."

Mary and Rebecca watched the older women walk off to bed, waiting until she was out of earshot before continuing their discussion.

"I just hope this does pan out," said Rebecca, "I don't see any way we're going to make it through a winter here."

Mary nodded. She had the same fears herself, fears that had been increasing as time went on.

"It's reminding me of the camps back on the island," she said, "it isn't anywhere near as bad, but..."

"But it will be," Rebecca interjected.

Mary remembered the last moments of the camp, carried by a soldier running from the infected, barely ahead of the inbound fighters and the resulting devastation.

"Yes, it will," she replied.

Rebecca leaned forward. "I think this is real. Make sure you and Joshua and Mrs. Andrews are ready for the evac. I have a feeling things are going to get rough around here when it happens." She paused, then continued. "Do you have a gun?"

Mary found herself surprised. She didn't, in fact, have a gun. Not that she was afraid of them or anything — she'd done pretty well on the range with her husband. She just hadn't felt the inclination — or had the opportunity — to obtain one.

"No," she answered.

Rebecca picked up her purse — more like a bag, thought Mary — and put it on her lap, rooting through it. Her hand emerged with a smallish black pistol.

"Can you shoot?" she asked.

"Yes," replied Mary, "I went to the range a few times with my husband."

"Can you handle this one okay?" asked Rebecca, holding up the pistol.

"Yes," replied Mary.

Rebecca ejected the magazine and ratcheted back the pistol's slide, then handed both to Mary.

"All yours."

Mary examined it and then put both on the coffee table.

"Really?" she asked.

"Better safe than sorry," said Rebecca.

Mary nodded. She'd been here before.

"One more thing," said Rebecca.

Mary nodded again.

"If this evacuation happens, we'll need to do triage at the hospital."

"We won't be taking terminal cases," said Mary.

"That's right," replied Rebecca. "This is only my prediction, but I'm pretty sure that North Bay's facilities won't be all that much better than ours. Those people we've been keeping comfortable as they die...we'll need to hurry along the process."

"Euthanize them," said Mary.

Rebecca nodded. "Like I said, that's my prediction. It's unpleasant, but resources are going to be limited all around. Tough decisions are going to be made."

Rebecca looked hard at Mary. "I wanted to make sure you're up to it."

Mary thought for a moment. Like a lifeboat, she mused, making sure there was room for her son, the people she cared about.

She nodded. "I'm up to it," she answered.

"I thought so," said Rebecca, "but I wanted to be sure."

"I'm sure," replied Mary.

Rebecca took a deep breath and blew it though her lips.

"I guess that's it then. I should get to the base, see if there are any new developments."

Rebecca stood and after a moment Mary did the same. The two walked to the door and Rebecca opened it. Mary could see the olive drab truck parked in the driveway. It seemed that Rebecca rated her own vehicle and wasn't subject to the curfew.

"Thanks, Rebecca," said Mary as she took the other woman's hand.

"You're welcome. Remember: be ready for it."

"I will. Goodbye."

"Goodbye, Mary."

Rebecca walked to the truck and Mary closed the door, walking over to the coffee table where the pistol lay. She stared at it for a moment before picking it and the magazine up. With a sigh, she inserted the magazine and pushed it home.

CHAPTER FOURTEEN

A Way Out

The latest argument with Morgan James involved the exact location where they'd park their caravan. James wouldn't, he told the man, move his people into the cleared houses along with the refugees. It would back his people into a corner, he said, and he made it quite clear that while great strides had been made, he still wasn't entirely comfortable with the new arrangements.

James' group had been on their own for long enough, the man thought, that they really only trusted themselves. They'd eventually come around, but in the meantime it wasn't a battle he was prepared to fight.

As a result, James' group had rolled their RVs and trailers inside the base's fencing, choosing an out of the way corner to park them. The soldiers took a liking to the hardened men and women and their families as word of their exploits against the infected spread throughout the troops. James' men — and women, in fact, equally competent and far more vicious in the face of attack — were treated to many a beer in the base's mess tent.

The man took to visiting James on a regular basis. He liked the gruff survivor, and valued his opinion on the situation they were in. Sometimes Harry went with him, and once or twice he'd brought Becky along. She'd confided with him afterward that she found James to be quite a charmer, "in a bit of a mountain-man kind of way".

Discussions and planning continued with North Bay, in the hope of some form of evacuation in the weeks to come. As Dawson had told the man, North Bay possessed four Hercules transport planes. Heavy lifters with a long range, more than able to reach them here and to transport them back — in a relay — to what sounded like safety.

Initial planning was for a maximum of two hundred people per flight. It would be uncomfortable, but doable. Of more concern was North Bay's request for food, fuel and armor. It was explained to the leaders here — an expanded group consisting of the man, Harry, Dawson, Rebecca and James — sitting around the radio, that a large influx of people would require extra supplies. On the surface, it sounded reasonable to the man, but it still felt uncomfortably like a price of admission.

"Why do they want the armored personnel carriers?" asked Becky after one call.

"They hardly have any armor at all," replied Dawson, "mostly aircraft and some infantry. The LAVs would help a lot in keeping them secure — run patrols, expand their perimeter. As we've found out. And it's easier to get them from us than to try to take them from some base that was overrun."

Most importantly, however, North Bay wanted the vaccine — preferably as soon as possible, even before the big transports started flying.

"It's a good idea," said the man to Rebecca, "having you and Dr. Hall somewhere safe. Safer than here, anyway."

"They don't need me," Becky replied, "Jeff can finish things off. We're close to production anyway."

The man admitted to himself that she was probably right, that Jeff Hall could take care of the final details, hand the equipment and research and instructions over to whatever counterparts he'd have in North Bay. And he admitted that his desire to get Becky out had at least something to do with his own personal reasons. Still.

"I could order you, you know," he said. He regretted it instantly.

She laughed. "Really?" She looked around. No one else was laughing. Dawson spoke.

"He could, Doctor."

Her laughter turned to consternation. "And who's supposed to take care of patients. Treat them until the evac starts, load them on planes, tend to them in flight?"

"There are others who can do that," replied Dawson. "Doctor," he continued, "I agree. You really do need to be one of the first ones out of here." She saw Harry nodding as well.

Becky glared at the man.

"Fine. I don't like it one bit, but fine."

The man knew that for the moment, he'd won. He also knew he'd be paying the price for it later.

"What about Mary?" asked Becky, later, when she and the man were alone.

"What about her?" replied the man.

"It might be useful to have her along on the trip."

"Becky," said the man with some exasperation, "it's nice of you to try to look after her. Lord knows Harry and I have, but there's absolutely no way any of us could justify it."

"But she's been a big help at the hospital, and maybe…"

"No, Becky. We're going to have a hard enough time managing those refugees out there. Imagine if they get a whiff of favoritism in the evacuation?"

Rebecca thought about his argument.

"Fine," she said, "you win. Again."

From her tone, the man didn't feel as if he'd won.

"I suppose I'd better start preparing," she said. "Telling Jeff about this is probably a good start. He won't be happy about it."

"He rarely is," muttered the man.

"Don't start," cautioned Rebecca. "Anyway," she continued, "I guess I have some time to get everything in order."

"Ummm," replied the man, "maybe not."

"What do you mean, 'maybe not'?" she demanded.

"Well," he said, "one of the ideas that's been floating around is to get you and Dr. Hall and the equipment to

North Bay as soon as possible. It's going to take us time to secure the runways at the airport for the Hercs to land."

"And?"

"And we're thinking that Charlottetown could probably get you close enough for North Bay to send a helicopter to collect you. Travel as far up the St. Lawrence as, say, Montreal. It'd be safe, and we could get you there quickly. Well, relatively quickly. And you'd be out of danger that much sooner."

Rebecca's eyes narrowed slightly at his last sentence.

"You're trying to protect me," she said, quietly.

The man realized he'd tripped himself up and was caught. He decided to answer honestly.

"I am, Becky. I've lost so many people that I care about…I guess I can't stand the thought of losing someone else."

The man was unable to read her expression or her reaction to his confession. He felt uncomfortable, waiting for some response.

Finally Becky's face broke into a smile and as she wrapped her arms around him, she whispered: "Don't worry, I'll be around for a long time."

Days went by, planning, organizing, the small group of leaders gradually expanding as their own expertise needed to be supplemented. Secrecy was still of the essence — this could all still fall through. Morale amongst the refugees, while not as bad as months ago in the earlier stages of the infection, wasn't exactly sky-high. Raising it with what might turn out to be false hope and then dashing it was something that the man and the others didn't want to risk.

"Something's come up that the troops, the ones enforcing curfew and working with the refugees have noticed," said Dawson as one of their meetings was winding down. "I didn't want to mention it until I got some confirmation and a clearer picture."

The others looked at him, waiting.

"Go ahead, Major," said the man.

Dawson nodded. "It seems as if some of the refugees have been disappearing. The troops started to notice this a few days ago. People who they'd see every day...they've stopped seeing them. And they've checked up on a few and the houses where they were placed and, well, they're empty."

"Empty? As in packed up and gone empty?" asked Harry. "Maybe they got tired of being cooped up, decided to head out on their own."

Dawson looked skeptical. "Could be," he said with a tone that implied that it couldn't, "but I'd be surprised at that. They haven't been cooped up, as you say, that long. And they're being well taken care of, and they know the risks outside."

"Do you have a theory?" asked the man.

Dawson shook his head. "I have a couple. I'd prefer not to share them until I have more information though."

"And your recommendation in the meantime?" asked the man. He too had an immediate, disturbing theory, but like Dawson, he'd keep it to himself for now.

"Keep an eye on things for the moment. It's a small number, but even so…it's troubling. I'll report back if and when I have more information."

"Okay Major," replied the man, "thanks for bringing this to everyone's attention."

Dawson nodded again.

"Any other business?" the man asked of the group in general. He hoped there wasn't. But of course there was.

Morgan James cleared his throat. The man sighed to himself.

"You have something, Mr. James?" asked the man.

"I do," replied James. He paused, then looked at Dawson. "Now I don't mean any disrespect to you or your troops, Major." Another pause. Dawson merely watched him, waiting. James continued. "I've been watching your patrols, and the way you have defenses set up and I was thinking: this is a pretty classic 'crust' defense, isn't it."

Dawson raised an eyebrow.

"I'm wondering," said James, "shouldn't you — or we — be running patrols outside? Keep an eye on what's going on so we don't get surprised?"

"We do patrol outside, Mr. James," replied Dawson.

James nodded. "You patrol the roads. What makes you think they're going to use the roads?"

'They,' thought the man, and remembered the infected he'd glimpsed on the way out of James' camp. A glimpse that he'd since convinced himself was imagination. Certainly not something to be worried about in the face of impending rescue, if that's what it ended up being.

"It's a good point," said the man.

Dawson thought for a moment. "It is a good point," he agreed.

"Now Major," said James, "I know your troops are spread thin, so there's only so much you can do. What I'm going to propose is that some of my folks go out, do some scouting, report back to you. They have the experience, you know."

Dawson looked at Harry, who nodded, then the man, who did the same. The phrase 'Indian Scouts' drifted though the man's head.

"I've heard good things about how your people conduct themselves in the field, Mr. James," he said, "I'd be happy to have you helping us out."

The man stood with Rebecca as they watched the last of the crates and equipment loaded into the Sea King. The man's emotions were conflicted: relief that Becky — and the vaccine — would soon be on their way to safety, and vague sadness at seeing her go. I've become more attached to her than I'd thought, the man mused.

As they watched, Jeff Hall rushed by, slowing down only to address Becky: "Time to go," he said, and then climbed into the waiting helicopter. He had, of course, said nothing to the man, who grimaced after Hall had gone by.

Becky turned to him, and he to her. She smiled at the lingering grimace he still wore.

"Think of it this way," she said, "you won't have to deal with him anymore, or even see him around."

The man grunted.

"I'll miss you, Becky," he said, "be careful."

"I don't think I have much to worry about," she replied, "I think you're the one who needs to be careful."

The man nodded. "Yeah, you're probably right."

Becky put her arms around the man, and he returned the embrace. It went on for a long time — long enough for the soldiers, finished with the loading of the helicopter, to notice and remark quietly to one another.

Finally, the man broke the embrace.

"You'd better get on," he said, "I'll be seeing you soon."

"You'd better," she said, and gave him a quick kiss. She turned and made her way to the helicopter's door, turning and waving to him before she climbed in. A soldier slid the door home and banged the side of the aircraft.

The man watched as the helicopter's blades began to turn, he and the soldiers moving out of the way of the aircraft's wash as it reached full power and then lifted off for the short trip out to Charlottetown, soon to begin the longer voyage up the St. Lawrence to the burned out city of Montreal.

The man followed the helicopter's flight until it diminished and then vanished before turning around and walking, feeling relieved, back to the command center. Maybe there was a shot at salvaging the Plan after all.

This would be the most dangerous time, thought the man as he drove to the airport, that period when they were spread so thin between the base and the refugees and the airport that problems which they'd dealt with easily in the past could become unmitigated disasters.

They recognized that, though, he and Harry and Dawson, and it stayed foremost in their thoughts as they organized the beginning of the evacuation.

The schedule for flying out the refugees had been the hardest part of the planning. Families first, had been the decision, and there was, predictably, some grumbling amongst those who were near the end of the roster. North Bay had been briefed on the potential situation and had assured them that they could handle the influx at their end. Remembering the camps on the island, the troops here would be the last to leave.

They hadn't, as yet, heard back from James and his crew, off scouting in the area around the base and the town. The man had mentioned it to Harry, who (he said) wasn't worried yet. After all, James' bunch had a lot of experience doing what they were doing. Give them a couple more days before starting to be concerned.

The man accepted this, but he still remembered the eyes he'd seen in the forest on the way back from James' camp.

The airport had been secured, and the requested supplies had been gathered — that last in itself a difficult enough task, but one that they would have had to undertake anyway, even without the pending evacuation. Fuel was a slightly different story, but the troops didn't take too long to figure out the airport's fueling arrangements. They would drain the airport dry by the final flight out.

It felt strange to drive directly up to the terminal building where troops and a pair of LAV's sat waiting. Harry met him when he exited the vehicle and voiced the same observation.

"No lineups at security, I take it?" Harry said, smiling.

The man laughed in response. "No, but I'd gladly go through one if I could get some decent coffee."

"Sorry," said Harry, "all we have is army issue."

The man laughed again.

"You're pretty upbeat today," said Harry, "something to do with Rebecca making it?"

The man nodded. "It's a big relief."

Harry smiled in response. "I'll bet it is."

"Not just for that reason, Harry," said the man. "She said on the radio that things look really good there. It's put some of my worries to rest."

"Now all we have to do is make it there ourselves," replied Harry.

Faintly, at first, but gradually growing louder, they could hear the sound of airplane engines.

"Right on time," said Harry.

Soon they saw the huge transport plane itself, flying low over the airport before disappearing again. The troops waved as it flew past.

"What's he doing?" asked the man.

"Making sure everything looks okay here," replied Harry. "He's checking that there aren't any threats. I understand his caution."

They saw the plane bank and circle, this time making its approach.

"Wheels are down," observed Harry, "I guess we pass inspection."

They watched as the transport gradually lowered until its wheels touched the runway, small puffs of dirt rising when contact was made. The plane decelerated, going past them again before slowing and making the turn towards the terminal and the waiting soldiers.

This would be the first flight out, carrying supplies to be used by the refugees. They would soon begin sending people — about two hundred at a time — intermixed with more supplies and, finally, the troops and their armor. North Bay had wanted the LAVs early on, but Dawson had convinced them of the need to keep the armor in place here as protection until the end.

"Get ready, folks," Harry said to the waiting troops, "he'll want to be loaded up and refueled as quickly as possible." The soldiers began to prepare for the exercise, starting up the fueling truck and moving the forklifts into position as the big plane moved closer to them. The man was surprised by just how massive the aircraft was as it neared them

The pilot of the plane waved to them as it approached. He seemed to wear a broad smile. The man waved back. So far, so good, he thought.

The plane came to a stop and the engines spun down. They heard the sound of the ramp opening, and moments later a crewman exited the aircraft, waving to the group. Harry and the man walked over to him.

"I see you folks are ready for us," the crewman said, "my name's McCabe — I'm the load master — I'll help you get everything stowed."

The man introduced himself and Harry. "The flight crew's staying on board, I'm guessing," said Harry.

McCabe nodded. "Orders. We're a little nervous about the situation here. As I'm sure you can imagine."

"I don't blame you," replied Harry, "anyway, let's get to it. Come on and I'll show you what we have for you."

Dusk was falling as the man drove back to the base. Well, he thought, the first flight went well. Let's hope all the rest of them do. Especially the ones with people on them.

He was stopped briefly at the gate rather than the usual wave-through.

"Major Dawson needs to see you immediately, sir," said the guard, when the man rolled down his window. The man had learned by now not to ask questions of soldiers relaying orders. The guard offered an answer anyway.

"Mr. James and his scouts are back, sir," said the young soldier. He looked worried. "I think they've found something, or found out about something. They didn't look too good." The soldier looked at the man questioningly. Of course he would, thought the man, after all, I'm 'in charge'.

"Thanks, Private," replied the man, more confidently than he felt, "whatever it is, I'm sure we can handle it. Remember, we won't be here forever We just have to keep everything together for a little while longer."

It might have been his imagination, but the soldier now seemed to look less nervous. More soldier-like, maybe.

"We will, sir. Thank you, sir," said the guard. The man nodded, rolled up his window and drove the short distance to the command post.

A small crowd milled about outside the building, illuminated by the exterior lights; some of James' men and women as well as troops. There was an animated conversation in progress as the man exited his vehicle. As he approached the building's door, the conversation stopped and heads turned towards him.

The man nodded to the people, standing, watching him. "Inside, I take it," he said.

One of the soldiers answered. "Yes, sir."

The man nodded again and walked through the door. He could feel the crowd's gaze on his back.

He found James in Major Dawson's office. The major looked shaken. Both men watched him silently as he entered the office.

"Better sit down," said Dawson. The man took a seat. Dawson looked at James. "Are you telling him, or am I?" he asked.

"Go ahead Major," replied James, "I'd rather not tell this story again for a while." Dawson nodded and turned to the man, looking at him for a moment before speaking.

"Mr. James has found our missing refugees."

CHAPTER FIFTEEN

End Plan

Mary awoke suddenly. A noise, she thought, although she couldn't put her finger on exactly what it was. She lay in bed, listening, waiting for it to repeat.

After a moment, she heard it again. A short rap on the front door. She heard Mrs. Andrews stir in the bedroom next to hers, presumably, she thought, to go to answer the door.

The rap again.

"I'm coming, I'm coming," she heard Mrs. Andrews call to the visitor or visitors on the other side of the door. Mary rolled over, opened the drawer of the night table next to her bed and removed the pistol Rebecca had given her. From another drawer she withdrew the clip and inserted it, then pulled back the slide to chamber a round. She couldn't have said why she felt the need to arm herself. She was probably being silly, she thought. But she kept the weapon in her hand as she got out of bed.

She heard Mrs. Andrews open the door, and then the voice of the older woman.

"Now what's this about —"

Mrs. Andrews' question was cut off by the sound of the door crashing open and the sound of commotion. A muted, liquid squawk from the older woman. Mary flicked the safety off her pistol and rushed out of her bedroom towards the front door.

Infected. A group of them; maybe four or five. Two carrying Mrs. Andrews like a rag doll, her head flopping aimlessly as they rushed her out the door.

The remaining infected focused on Mary, animal cunning in their eyes. They moved towards her. Mary raised the pistol and set her sights on the nearest one. As she squeezed off the shot, some part of her was amazed by the calmness that had overcome her.

The first infected dropped, her shot hitting it in the chest. The others — two more — hesitated and then resumed moving towards her. She fired twice more. Rapidly, without thinking. They dropped to join the first, a trail of bodies almost reaching her.

Mary took a deep breath and looked at the infected lying on the floor. She moved slowly towards them. One was still alive, eying her with hatred. She thought of Joshua upstairs as she shot it in the head and then turned to look at the door through which Mrs. Andrews had vanished. She moved towards it — slowly, cautiously — and reaching it, peered out into the darkness.

At first she could see nothing, but as her eyes adjusted she could make out movement down the street. Silhouettes, running between the houses. She heard screams and bursts of gunfire and before she closed and bolted the door, the sound of a siren in the distance.

"Eating them," said the man flatly, still trying to process what he'd just been told.

James nodded. "It looked like a butcher's shop. Hanging from the beams in the barn like cattle carcasses."

The man felt the gorge rising in his throat. He swallowed before asking the next question.

"How many?"

"Lots," replied James. "We didn't count them all," he added quietly.

Dawson, who until now had been watching the man's reaction, spoke up.

"We need to step up the evacuation," he said, "we're spread too thin to protect the airport and the base and the refugees."

The man nodded. "Have you advised North Bay?"

"No," replied Dawson, "I was waiting for you. I'm going to suggest moving everything to the airport — the refugees, the troops, the armor, everything. It'll be uncomfortable for everyone, but it's the best chance to pull this off without a disaster."

The man nodded again. "Let's do it, Major."

They sat quietly together for a moment, each reflecting on this new situation. Like cattle, thought the man: we've built them a fine little farm to harvest.

The sound of a siren jolted the three to alertness. The man sighed inwardly. This wouldn't be good, he thought.

A hurried knock on the door before it swung open, a soldier, not waiting for an invitation to enter.

"Sir," said the young women, visibly struggling to hold her composure, and doing so admirably, "we have a situation with the refugees."

Troops boiled through the streets, knocking on doors and comforting residents, squads examining trails left by the raiding infected. Too many trails, marked with blood and the violent struggles of those who had been carried off still alive.

Harry arrived as Dawson and the man stood surveying the situation.

"Jesus," he said, viewing the scene for the first time.

"Yeah," replied the man.

"Are we going after them?" asked Harry.

Dawson shook his head, still watching the troops, before replying.

"No."

"No?" said Harry, an incredulous note in this voice.

"No. We're evacuating everyone to the airport and getting the hell out of here while we can."

"You agreed with that?" Harry asked the man.

"Yeah."

"But—" started Harry.

"You missed Morgan James' debrief, Major," interrupted Dawson, "they're harvesting us."

The man watched the color drain out of Harry's face as he processed Dawson's statement. "You mean—" began Harry.

"I mean, Major, that they've been raiding us, capturing our people, killing them and, yes, eating them. That's what I mean."

"Jesus," said Harry.

Dawson nodded. "Exactly." The man said nothing, barely listening to the exchange as he watched the troops at work. He had a bad feeling. He turned to face the two officers.

"Gentlemen," he said, "let's get this operation started. Now."

North Bay was nervous. Very nervous.

In extended radio contact with them, Dawson and the man explained the new situation and requested that the airlift be accelerated. The man could hear the hesitation on the other end of the radio connection. North Bay already had the vaccine, and he could hear the decision on whether or not they needed the armor being weighed in their voices. They certainly didn't need the extra people — extra mouths to feed that may or may not belong to someone who'd be useful in the new world. And they didn't want to risk their transports and personnel in what looked to be turning into a very hot zone indeed.

The man resisted the urge to attempt to pull rank — mostly because he didn't think it would work, and he didn't want to trigger the collapse of the remaining structure, even if it might only be an illusion.

In the end, decency and responsibility and honor prevailed. North Bay would run the Hercs around the clock until the evacuation was complete. And an added bonus.

"We're sending air support," they said.

The logistics were horrible, but they'd put a pair of tankers up to let the fighters reach them and continue a patrol, performing overwatch on the evacuation operation. They'd dispatch them immediately.

The man turned to Dawson after they'd signed off.

"Major," he said, "we just might be okay." Their chances of survival had just improved, he thought, but if he was right, they had to move fast.

The man watched as soldiers herded refugees onto trucks. Herded, he thought, the irony not lost on him. He saw fear in the faces of the people, intensifying in some of them as their eyes were drawn to the blood trails that seemed to be everywhere.

Harry was supervising the refugee transport, while Major Dawson was shuttling between the base and the airport, ensuring that a solid defensive perimeter was established. The man thought they would need it before the end.

The scene paused suddenly as everyone — the soldiers and refugees both — stopped to look up and watch the Hercules pass low overhead, making its approach to the airport. The first transport; North Bay's word had been good, and now all they had to do here was get the people on them.

The man saw Harry and walked over to him.

"How goes it?" he asked.

Harry glanced at him. "So far, so good. As long as there isn't any panic, we should have everyone moved to the airport in—" Harry glanced at his watch "—let's say, six hours."

"Before dark then."

Harry nodded. "With some room to spare."

The bottleneck, as they'd discussed, would be the planes themselves. Even flying around the clock, the big Hercs wouldn't be able to move everyone until the next morning at best. They'd have to hold the airport until then.

"There's Mary," said Harry, pointing to a long line of people waiting to board a truck. The man looked to where Harry gestured, and saw Mary with Joshua in hand, waiting patiently. He'd heard about her experience the night before. Unlike most of the others standing with her, Mary's face was grim, and there was an air of determination about her. She certainly wasn't the same girl he'd first met back in Alma, he thought.

Another Hercules passed overhead.

"You heard that Morgan James and his crew bugged out this morning?" asked Harry.

"Yeah," replied the man, "he really doesn't have too much faith in us, does he."

Harry chuckled. "No," he said, "and you know, he'll probably make out just fine wherever he and his bunch end up."

"Yeah."

Another Hercules.

Close to two thousand people to fly out, not to mention any supplies they could pack on board and the armor that North Bay still wanted.

"I'm going to head over to the airport," said the man. "See how Dawson is making out."

Harry nodded. "See you in a while."

The man arrived at the airport just as the first Hercules was taking off, loaded with refugees. A cordon of troops stood evenly spaced at the fence surrounding the field, armed and in their full kit, the armored personnel carriers interspersed among them with cannon facing outward.

A soldier directed the man to where Major Dawson was located, overseeing the loading of the next plane.

"Major," said the man by way of greeting.

Dawson nodded. "We're packing them in like sardines," he said, watching the surprisingly orderly loading process. "It's not going to be a very pleasant trip."

"More pleasant than being here," said the man. Dawson grunted in agreement.

The man gestured upwards at the fighters orbiting high above the airfield. "Anything from them?" he asked.

"Nothing," replied Dawson, "yet."

The plane had finished loading and the ramp slowly lifted into position. Once the fueling truck had moved out of the way, its engines revved up and it began to move off the apron towards the runway.

"Two down," observed Dawson as the next plane began to move into place.

The sound of jet fighters increased from background noise to a deafening roar as two fighters suddenly dropped out of orbit and headed low towards the fence and gate at high speed. At the same time, Dawson's radio squawked.

"Major, we have incoming," the man heard.

"Shit," said Dawson. He yelled at the soldier supervising the loading of the next plane. "Get that done fast!" The soldier saluted and moved to speed up the loading process.

They heard the sound of rifle fire, mixed with the machine guns and cannon from the LAVs. A blast from a bomb, presumably from one of the fighters.

"Get on that plane," said Dawson to the man.

The remaining fighters screamed towards the town where Harry was still trying to move the refugees to the airport.

"No," replied the man, "I'm going back to town."

"You're a fool then," said Dawson, and saluted the man. "Good luck," he said.

"And you, Major," said the man, returning the salute as best he could. A truck pulled up, screeching to a halt. Dawson got in the passenger's side and it left as quickly as it had arrived. The man saw Dawson checking his sidearm as he drove away.

More explosions and more gunfire as the man got into his own vehicle and headed towards the gate. Soldiers were engaging infected — hundreds of them. Even with the armament on their side, they'd soon be overwhelmed. The man silently wished them luck and pushed the truck to its limit as he sped out of the gate towards town.

The man passed two trucks on the way into town. Both were stopped, the ground around them littered with bodies and blood. He didn't stop as he sped by. He also resisted the urge to look into the back of the trucks as he passed.

The staging area in the town was the scene of a slaughter. He saw a group of soldiers and civilians huddled together under cover and headed for them. The sound of jets pounding positions nearby was deafening.

As he arrived, he saw that Harry was one of the soldiers. And Mary and Joshua were with the group of civilians, Mary holding a rifle. The man felt relief and, immediately after that, shame for feeling that relief when so many others hadn't made it.

He counted twenty people. After everything, he thought, this was what they were down to.

"Harry!" he yelled over the roar of the jets and the blasts of the bombs.

Harry motioned him over and the man moved quickly to him, hunkering down at Harry's side.

"The airport's gone," said Harry, "we need to leave. The fighters aren't going to be able to hold them back here much longer."

Go where, thought the man. He nodded instead.

Harry pointed at a group of parked trucks and Jeeps. The man looked at them and nodded again. Harry yelled into his radio, and the bombing seemed to intensify. He yelled to the other soldiers and they began to move, marshaling the civilians.

They ran towards the vehicles and scrambled around them, finding seats as quickly as they could until finally everyone was in place. Although it took seconds, it felt like forever. As they drove off, the man saw one of the jets fly directly over their heads and waggle its wings as if saying goodbye.

CHAPTER SIXTEEN

Epilogue

The man stood at the edge of the ocean and gazed out over the grayish-blue water, the sound of the waves hitting the beach around him steady and hypnotic. The beach was long and narrow, following the curve of the shoreline in both directions as far as the eye could see, weaving gently in and out of tiny bays, a ribbon of vaguely reddish sand set against the straw color of late summer grasses. There were still hundreds more miles they needed to travel before they'd reach safety, but the flight of the last few days had taken their toll and he badly needed to rest.

"No time for that now," said Harry, approaching him from behind. "Are you ready to move on?"

The man turned around, the illusion of solitude broken as the small party entered his view, standing beside the motorcycles they'd traded their trucks and Jeeps for. Mary saw him looking and waved, rifle slung over her shoulder.

"Yeah," replied the man, taking one last look at the ocean and thinking that, at least this time, he wouldn't be alone. "Let's go."

www.ingramcontent.com/pod-product-compliance
Lightning Source LLC
Chambersburg PA
CBHW022008170626
46808CB00001B/323